Edited by John Metcalf

Best Canadian Stories
15

The publishers acknowledge the support of the Canada Council for the Arts, the Government of Ontario through the Ontario Media Development Corporation and the Government of Canada through the Canada Book Fund for their publishing activities.

"Knife Party" by Mark Anthony Jarman was first published in *Prairie Fire* and a much shorter version of "Pompeii Book of the Dead" appeared in *Descant*; "Palace of the Brine" by Kerry-Lee Powell originally appeared in *The Malahat Review* after winning their Far Horizons Award; "Marriage" by Rebecca Rosenblum and "Wasaga500" by Megan Findlay were first published in *The New Quarterly*; "The Dog and the Sheep" by Cynthia Flood first appeared in *Numéro Cinq*; "Rhubarb" by Lauren Carter was originally published in *Prairie Fire* after winning first prize in their fiction contest; "Old Man Marchuk" by Kevin Hardcastle was first published in *Event*; "The Historian" by Leon Rooke originally appeared in *The Antioch Review*; "Scottish Annie" by Alice Petersen was first published in *The Fiddlehead*.

The following magazines were consulted: *The Antigonish Review*, *The Capilano Review*, *The Danforth Review*, *Descant*, *Event*, *Exile*, *The Fiddlehead*, *Geist*, *Grain*, *The Malahat Review*, *Matrix*, *The New Quarterly*, *Prairie Fire*, *PRISM international* and *subTerrain*.

ISBN 978 0 7780 1431 7 (hardcover)
ISBN 978 0 7780 1432 4 (softcover)
ISSN 0703 9476

Book design by Michael Macklem
Printed in Canada

PUBLISHED IN CANADA BY OBERON PRESS

 Canada Council   Conseil des Arts   Canada
for the Arts   du Canada

Contributions for the forty-sixth volume, published or unpublished, should be sent to Oberon Press, 205–145 Spruce Street, Ottawa, Ontario KIR 6PI *before 31 March, 2016. All manuscripts should enclose a stamped self-addressed envelope.*

Reading in the literary magazines during 2015, I noticed an advertisement placed by the journal *Studies in Canadian Literature/Études en littérature canadienne* calling for the submission of papers under the general heading *Canadian Literature: The Past Forty Years*, for an issue of the journal celebrating its fortieth anniversary.

The words "Canadian literary scholarship" provoked a horse laugh.

The advertisement continued:

"The period witnessed substantial developments and shifts in the field, from the legitimation of Canadian literature as an academic field of study and the rise of popular non-academic phenomena such as 'Canada Reads' and the Giller Prize, to significant literary and critical movements, postmodernism, postcolonialism, feminism, canon debates, new historicism, Indigenous studies, book history, transnationalism, critical race theory, queer studies, diaspora studies, and more recently, advances in the fields of digital humanities and ecocriticism."

What a doomed and deadening recital!

Not a whisper about the Nobel Prize for Literature.

Not a word about art or the rhetorics necessary to achieve it, not a word about aesthetic success, not a word about the vision and passion that aesthetic concerns serve.

Daunting though the effort would be, one should, perhaps, try to summon compassion.

While Canadian literary scholars have been for the last 40 years seeding the blighted crops of "ecocriticism," "indigenous studies," "queer studies" and "critical race theory," here at Oberon we are celebrating with this volume the forty-fifth anniversary of the *Best Canadian* anthology, which both seeds *and* harvests. We promote no 'ism,' school or ideology. We fight under the banner of the question Mavis Gallant asked of all the arts: *Is it dead or alive?*

Under the editorial eyes of David Helwig, Tom Marshall, Joan Harcourt, Clark Blaise, Leon Rooke, Maggie Helwig, Sandra

Martin, and Douglas Glover, Oberon's *Best Canadian Stories* has for 45 years championed the Best (how "Canadian literary scholars" hate that word!) and sought out and nurtured promising newcomers. Even in the uncertain early days, the contents pages were stellar.

In 1976: Norman Levine, Hugh Hood, Audrey Thomas, Clark Blaise, Elizabeth Spencer, and Leon Rooke.

In 1978: Alice Munro, Hugh Hood, Elizabeth Spencer.

In 1980: Mavis Gallant, Alice Munro, Guy Vanderhaeghe, and a first published story from Linda Svendsen who would go on to write the shimmering collection *Marine Life*.

As the years rolled on we published: Diane Schoemperlen, Libby Creelman, Caroline Adderson, Mark Anthony Jarman, Douglas Glover, Annabel Lyon, Elise Levine, Ann Copeland, Dayv James-French, Terry Griggs, Steven Heighton, K.D Miller, Keath Fraser, Mary Borsky, Elizabeth Hay, Antanas Sileika, Mary Swan, Andrew Pyper, Michael Winter, Mike Barnes, Sharon English...and my editorial eye is currently caressing Kevin Hardcastle, Alice Petersen, Kathy Page....

About a decade ago, the literary columnist Philip Marchand wrote in the *Toronto Star*:

"There is something both heartening and disheartening about the fact that so much of the strength of Canadian literary culture lies in the short story form. It is heartening because there are now many Canadian writers who are truly proficient in the art— so much so that whatever is enduring in our literature will be more likely found in their work than in over-stuffed prose epics such as [Rohinton Mistry's] *A Fine Balance* or [Timothy Findley's] *The Piano Man's Daughter*.

The situation is in some respects similar to Elizabethan and Jacobean England, where a cultural climate favoured the production of an enormous amount of good lyric verse, sonnets, and so on. Most of this good verse has since been classified by academic critics as 'minor' but it was wonderful minor stuff and it has remained undimmed by time.

Something similar may be said about Canadian short fiction in the late twentieth century. The disheartening element in the situation, of course, is that few people actually read it."

The accuracy of Marchand's remarks cannot be gainsaid but

8

I will offer again the assertions I made in the Introduction to the 1977 volume:

"An anthology such as this offers some slight hope, It offers to a larger audience work that otherwise might well not have been seen; it extends the life of a piece of work; it directs the attention of readers to writers who otherwise might have been consigned to the vaults on microfilm.

The editorial task is not merely one of compilation; it is also critical. Frank Kermode described literary criticism as 'the medium in which past work survives'. We hope that this anthology and succeeding ones will serve this function as well as offering immediate pleasure."

Can we keep on making such assertions in the face of indifference and against the hostility to art implied in 'digital humanities and ecocriticism', 'queer studies', and 'critical race theory'?

Oh, yes! Our editors remain hunched at the edge of the frontiers watching the swirling gravel for hints of gold. Hard to find and correspondingly treasured, rust-proof, impervious to the attack of acid, beautiful. Makes its way into the hands of the few. After that...?

The other night, sitting under a pool of lamp-light, I was re-reading, simply for pleasure, some stories I hadn't visited in years. They're over 60 years old now, those first stories of Truman Capote's, the stories in *Other Voices, Other Rooms* and *The Tree of Night*.

Many years ago, when I was teaching myself how to read, these stories were Capote's gift to me...handed on in the endless process of handing on.

You Ever See the Snow?

"'You ever see the snow?'

Rather breathlessly Joel lied and claimed that he most certainly had; it was a pardonable deception, for he had a great yearning to see bona-fide snow; next to owning the Koh-i-noor diamond, that was his ultimate secret wish. Sometimes, on flat boring afternoons, he's squatted on St. Deval Street and daydreamed silent pearly snowclouds into sifting coldly through the boughs of the dry, dirty trees. Snow falling in August and

9

silvering the glassy pavement, the ghostly flakes icing his hair, coating rooftops, changing the grimy old neighborhood into a hushed frozen white wasteland uninhabited except for himself and a menagerie of wonderbeasts: albino antelopes, and ivory-breasted snowbirds: and occasionally there were humans, such fantastic folk as Mr. Mystery, the vaudeville hypnotist, and Lucky Rogers, the movie star, and Madame Veronica, who read fortunes in a Vieux Carré tearoom. 'It was one stormy night in Canada that I saw the snow,' he said, though the farthest north he'd ever set foot was Richmond, Virginia."

I'm just saying....

JOHN METCALF

Knife Party and Pompeii
Book of the Dead
Mark Anthony Jarman

Clouds pile high over the Vatican like horses biting each other, clouds rising over Rome's glowing peach walls and tiles and television antennas. One white gorgeous mushroom cumulus lifts higher and higher—I love looking at it, staring into the ruins of this God-like face.

The blue Italian night turns darker and darker and a stranger's ebony piano plays near my flowered terrace. Rome or Naples or Pompeii: a piano trills or a dog barks somewhere near me, perhaps the apartment across the way. A sense opens inside my brain or ear and needs to know where the sound is formed, to know more of this mysterious envoy from another home.

At home in Canada our household is divided, literally and figuratively.

Turns out I don't have room for the oak bookcases, my wife says on the phone, but I'd like to keep the big quilt.

Okay, I agree.

And the car.

Okay.

You can have the roll-top desk.

Okay.

I, the bad husband, find myself agreeing to anything. In Rome that divided home seems so far away.

South of Napoli our train speeds into the side of an Italian mountain and we have no eyesight, we knife noisily into black tunnels and then shoot out again, our new eyes viewing the patient volcano and ancient sea.

Our noisy engine halts its iron wheels at sea-side towns where families alight with beach towels and fashionable sunglasses and sunburns that still have hours to flare into ripeness.

The train's exit doors have small windows, but they do not open and the cars are furnace hot. Tough kids from the illegal burbs built on the slopes of the volcano stand in an alcove where there are no seats, beside the exit doors.

Into light and out. In the confines of a dark tunnel something incredibly fractious and noisy grinds against our train and the tunnel walls that hug us. The windows are open to roaring air, open to relieve the incredible heat, and this new clamour makes all the passengers flinch and panic, metal debris bouncing and crashing and wrenching our heat-stroke dreams. What the hell is hitting the curved shell of our train?

In the alcove the sketchy teenagers are moving shadows and I make out one lithe shadow leap mightily to kick out a window in the train's exit door. The teens attack the door's sealed window when the train is in a tunnel; they think no-one sees them in the blackness.

One kid swings nimbly on a high chrome bar, a true acrobat who, with both feet, hits the window hard, a human battering ram, and more fragments of glass and metal frame break away in the dark to clatter and bounce along the shell of the rocketing train.

Our train bursts out of the tunnel and they stop smashing the window and pose casually in mad light. In the next tunnel the kicking starts again.

Wives look to their husbands: will you do something? Each husband shrugs. Polizia ride many trains, but not today. Where is the stoic conductor?

The Italian teens try to look cool in huge mirrored aviator shades, but their faces are so thin and the aviator glasses so large—the effect is of Clownish Child rather than Top Gun or Corrupt Saigon Major. I react primitively at times like this; I know they carry knives, but I'd like to trash *them* the way they trash their own train, our train, see how they like it. But I know we'll all be elsewhere soon if we just wait and do nothing.

I should just sit, but I walk to the alcove and stand beside the cretins so they will stop destroying the door. My move was not well thought out. There are more of them in the hormonal antechamber than I realized and sullen girls lean in the mix. I wish I was a more confident vigilante man with amazing eye-hand coordination and hidden weapons. They look to each other for guidance in child-thug matters. No-one steps forward to test my skill set, my tennis elbow. Uncertain moments hang, served to us like writs.

The gang clambers off at the next stop, pushing and shoving each other out the doors with high spirits. *Ah youth; how I hate them.* The damaged doors open for the rabble, but then the doors won't close. Now the arthritic train can't move. The stoic conductor examines the doors, tries to heal them in the heat. He wears a dark blue uniform, but seems unaffected by the climate, while sweat falls from my sleeves. The conductor and another Italian man work to coax the doors to close.

On the station platform I see my cousin Eve and Tamika with the gang that smashed the doors. Why get off the train here? For pancakes and syrup? This is not our stop. I leap from the carriage just as the afflicted doors finally close and the train and conductor shunt away without me. The station sign and walls are covered with day-glo graffiti imitating American style tags; a new empire paints over an old empire.

"Hey!" calls my cousin Eve. "I met these Italian guys at the beach. This is Giorgio and Peppino and Santino. They invited me to a party. For real. Want to come with?"

Tamika says, "Not me, I'm going back to the hotel." Tamika is shy and she is smart.

"Hey, you come with me." My cousin Eve takes my arm. "Please!"

I have a bad feeling; I don't want to go to this party, but I don't want Eve to go alone.

My cousin says, "We can buy cold beer here at the station."

"You will come?" says Santino from the beach. "It's a very nice apartment, a very nice freaking party. Yes, you may enjoy it."

In a line we pass the military base and pass rows of monochrome flats, pedestrians in a drab hidden Italy, party to an Italy that has little to do with tourist brochures and silk suits and genius marble. We walk inland away from the sea, around a hill and past a canal and cluster of Chinese factories and a military base with dark green tanks, World War Two vintage tanks hunched like guardians either side of the gate. A fat bee accompanies us for a few moments.

We hear the party before finding stairs like a ladder up into a crowd spilling into a dim hall and filling a living-room and kitchen. In the living-room leans a pole lamp with a blue light bulb, so we all look reasonably unhealthy, and every surface crammed with glasses, ashtrays, vats of red wine, cloudy Ouzo, grappa, tins of German lager, and green bottles of Italian beer.

Past the pink sofa hides an invisible but loud stereo: Jesus and Mary Chain ply distorted fuzz-box ditties. Are Jesus and Mary Chain still churning out discs? I liked them when I was younger; funny to hear them in this other world. A circle is smoking dope and a young woman is coughing up a lung. The fuming joint finds its way to us. I feel nothing at first.

A man flashes a glassine envelope of coke to the young woman. A neighbour, we are told, he lives across the hall, a party crasher attracted by the crowd, the women. The neighbour is not invited, he is not welcome, he does not carry himself well.

"Come stai?"

"You are from America?"

"I'm not from America."

"Yes, you are."

"No, Canada."

"That's much better culture."

"Bene."

"So, Mister Canada, do you like Napoli?"

"Si, Mister Italy, certo, very much, molto simpatico, it's amazing."

"Mister Canada calls me Mister Italy. Ha ha ha."

The unwelcome neighbour offers coke on his wrist to the younger woman, he says, "My coke is very fine. Just think, all the way from Ecuador to Napoli and to your pretty nose. Think of that. I bring it here in crates of bananas."

"Don't listen to his big talk," says Mister Italy. "He doesn't bring it."

"You should watch your fat mouth."

14

"Bananas!" says my cousin. "Bananas have big hairy spiders! I hate spiders!"

I know Eve's phobia, my cousin is very serious about this fear, as if spiders are hiding now in the small amount of coke. I wonder if I could get some of that product. I drink cold beer I bought at the train station. The party crasher neighbour with the coke is after the women. Like me.

Mister Italy tells him to leave. Mister Italy turns away, the neighbour sucker punches Mister Italy, and the young man drops, holding his face.

"Get out!" shout Santino and the others. They insult the neighbour, slap him, push him out the door to go back to his apartment. He crosses the narrow hall; all the doors are wide open.

My cousin looks at the table as if there might be spiders there.

"That cake," she asks me. "Is that icing or mould? It looks like mould."

"I'm going with icing," I say and take some.

"Eew, I can't believe you ate that."

"I'm starving."

A young man in a foetal position rocks in the corner, arms hugging his knees. Three women look bored. They are all younger than me, the new norm; now I am always the oldest person present as music plays loudly and the wild ones turn this way and that, shouting into songs and bright conversations.

One stoned woman walks past with a half-open blouse, breast curves greatly revealed. Rare once to see a lady's bare ankle. Blouses open wide and life goes on. A startling bright blue vein runs down one breast to disappear into her blouse. Bright as a streak of blue paint or a cobalt serpent and she is so happy to make public the blood pulsing in her vein.

My high school girlfriend worried about veins on her high school breasts. Your breasts are beautiful, I tried to reassure her, but she worried about a vein. And this Italian girl so happy to show off the bright vein on her breast, blood moving inside her breast. Blood is red as wine so why is a vein blue? Why am I blue? I wish to be captivating: is that too much to ask?

The neighbour motors back from his apartment carrying a staple gun, crosses the hall, crosses the room, and puts the staple gun to Mister Italy's thigh, driving in a heavy duty staple. Mister Italy leaps, tears springing out of his eyes, Mister Italy flees the room yelling and cursing.

"I'm worried about him."

"Is he all right?"

"Does he even know his way?"

"To what?"

The stoned woman disappears down the hall of muffled echoes. Later she comes back to the sofa and says to my cousin, "Don't worry."

I try to not study her sea-blue vein, though I find it fascinating and would pay money to look carefully and touch it, but I do not believe she would be interested in such an examination.

The neighbour wanders into the kitchen, still wielding the staple gun. Everyone in the kitchen is shouting normally. I stand up. The party in the living-room rages on around me, roller coaster voices, the droning fuzz-tone of Jesus and Mary Chain picking up speed and slowing down. I sit down.

The stoned young woman with the cobalt vein on her breast dances jerkily in the living-room, blouse now completely asunder, her skin taking in the air, the last button no longer intimate with eyelet, free. I assume Cobalt Girl is aware of her blouse and breasts out there like vivid menus, though who knows. Above her neck hovers her very own brain, choreographing her dance in our music and shouting.

My cousin pins her mouth to my ear. I enjoy her mouth at my ear.

"What?" I whisper into her warm ear.

"Have you noticed?" My cousin directs my gaze with her eyes.

This young woman's brown nipples are extremely thin and long, like tiny twigs, where a bird might perch. Now, would milk squirt a greater distance farther from such narrow nipples? A question of physics, pressure. And my cousin's nipples so tiny and pale pink glimpsed once in a hotel room, in repressed memory. Forget that image.

Cobalt Girl dances with Santino, dances with elbows close to her waist, hands and wrists outward as she shimmies, almost The Twist. I would like to start a new dance craze. Do the

Mashed Potato. Do the Staple Gun, do The Lazy Lawyer, do the Dee-vor-cee dividing his assets.

Santino grins at me, Santino whispers in her ear and they dance some more and then they stop.

"You must watch, my new friends," says Santino. "In an American movie we saw a dancer do this."

The other, is his name Pepini? Penino? My brain is not to be relied on. Where is my drink.

Santino takes one paper match and splits the middle of the match so that there is an opening. Cobalt Girl takes the match from Santino and carefully places the opening of the one match to her breast so that the match grips her long nipple. Santino hands her another such match.

She lights both matches, pointing the head up and away from her skin, then Cobalt Girl dances proudly in front of us, shifting her hips and smiling at her party trick.

She says something in Italian.

"Do you see this in Canada?" Santino translates.

"No."

"No, I thought not. Not in Canada, eh."

Is that an Italian eh or a Canadian eh?

The stoned woman dances and moves her head side to side, she's seen this sultry style of dancing on videos, moves so that her hair swings about like a star on celluloid. I was worried about the small flames hurting the skin of her breasts, but instead the burning matches cause her swinging hair to catch on fire, perhaps a tad too much flammable hairspray or some weird gel.

My cousin Eve says, That isn't good, and she points a finger like a gun.

Santino looks from us to Cobalt Girl, stops grinning and calmly throws his drink on her, so I pour the remainder of my beer over her burning hair and others add their drinks. It is as if we are allowed to urinate on her. Cobalt Girl is crying, tears and drinks tracking down over her breasts and snuffed black matches, Cobalt Girl runs to the bathroom, hair smoking like a volcano. It's kind of sexy. Where is the volcano, I mean the washroom? Where am I?

Sometimes when travelling I must look about and remind myself where I am, what country I gaze at. I like that feeling of being momentarily lost, of a brief gap, of having different eyes, new eyes upon old trees and the brightest scooter. I am near Napoli on a scratchy pink couch and I am opening a beer that is now warm. Sometimes I feel like that dead Roman rat I saw beneath the trees. Sometimes I feel like a chocolate bar with too many bite marks. Sometimes I feel the world is a very beautiful white T-shirt.

Another giant joint makes the rounds, strong and harsh behind my teeth. I feel instantly stoned or re-stoned, I'm not sure, not used to this quality. Eve says that Mister Italy is back. By the door a teenager from the train is showing Santino and Mister Italy a knife with a beautiful handle the shade of dark honey, as if an ancient insect might be trapped there in amber. They admire the knife.

The woman with hair once on fire is laughing, though her hair looks frizzily fucked up: she moves room to room laughing, smoking up from a tiny bag of weed.

She says to me in Italian, "After that ordeal I am thirsty, tell me, do you have birra?"

"Si. Yes. I'm happy to share."

"That's good you are happy with me." Cobalt Girl smiles, puts on a porkpie hat, just a girl who likes the traditional drugs. It may be the fine dope, but her laughing makes me laugh.

I'm not happy, but I know I can be happy again. I know it is there, but what port of call, what passport, what bright map on my wall, what coast and sea? I know a port exists, know it is close. When I find it I will write a book called Duct Tape for the Soul and it will sell millions.

"Thank you for the birra."

"Prego. De nada." Or is that Spanish? I get them mixed up, think I'm back in Spain. I wonder if Cobalt Girl was with the group kicking out the train window. She mimes tossing beer on her hair. Si. She mimes a moonwalk. Michael Jackson! Yes! I get it now. His hair burnt too!

The kitchen group fights as if one pulsating organism. Perche vendichi su di me l'offesa che ti ha fatto un altro? Why are you taking revenge on me for someone else's offence? It sounds too

Sicilian for words. Why are they all so fucking loud?

The white doorway pours noise into the living-room; young males run out and males run into the kitchen talking in tongues, raucous Italian voices producing a rapid clatter of words, like a rock beach rolling in brisk surf.

Mamma mia, che rabbia mi fai! How you enrage me!

Mi trattengo dal dire quello che penso solo per buona educazione. I refrain from saying what I think only because of my good upbringing.

Santino has a silver pen, or is it the knife? What is he saying to Mister Italy?

I will kill him. Hands waving. To give a lesson.

In the kitchen dozens are shoving each other, pushing and fighting, two sides, three sides, one room of the party becoming a minor brawl.

A young woman says something and is knocked over and kicked by the older neighbour and she crawls the floor like a shouting crocodile. Maybe this is normal, I can't tell as there is so much noise in Italy, so much life, so many scooter horns beeping threats and throats calling out la dolce vita, vim and vengeance, someone shouting *dare una lezione*, give him a lesson, a leg for a leg.

During the day they shout at me at the grocery, at the cashier, at the café, in the street, from the kitchen; it's almost comic to be shouted at so much. What leg? Mister Italy's leg? I start to stand up, but the stoned woman laughs and pushes me down into someone's lap. From my odd perspective I have a sideways view of the crowded kitchen.

Santino bends low, his face looking so sleepy, swings his arm low in a resigned arc that ends with a knife driven into the older man's thigh. Blood gushes immediately at the base of the knife, as if Santino struck an oil well and in the room a general hiss of understanding and pity and then more voices, more shouting, more gesturing. His leg, his blood splattered denim, blood falls from him, blood on the floor, smeared on the white fridge.

Santino runs out of the crowd like a hunched assassin. Mister Italy and others follow him out the door in a more assured manner. Staple Gun Guy looks at his liquid leg. The knife is gone from his leg. Who took the knife?

Maybe the assailant thought a jab to the leg was not dangerous, but the blood wells, pours from him, blood born in the kitchen, he can't stop the blood freed from culverts and tunnels. The blood is dark, but glistening at the same time. Blood polka dots around the kitchen, dots the size of coins, red coins painted everywhere so quickly. How can there be so much blood draining from one cut? The eye can't understand the image it seizes (*I smote him thus*).

He stares at his leg, nature staring back at you. The stoned woman holds a tea towel to the gushing leg. "It won't stop!"

The long knife must have met an artery, severed an artery, we meet in a rented room of blood, blood so scarlet on their white floor and dark rug and a trail as he heads to the door, to another country. The neighbour wishes to go home with his staple gun. It's my party and I'll die if I want to.

He passes and my cousin and I stare as if a monster is walking past on a moor (*amore!*). The monster passes the armchair the shape and colour of an ancient tombstone and the coffee table with my bottles and the small baggy of cocaine under the blue light bulb. My cousin says he shouldn't walk if he's bleeding like that.

The neighbour makes it to the door, but in the hall falls like a Doric column. He has bled out. Now the kitchen empties, groups pushing and shoving, not to fight, but to exit. Partygoers nimbly leap his body blocking the doorway and flee like goats down the long hall. An older woman opens her apartment door to peer out at the raucous stampede, the mad stomping hurdle race. Spying blood and a body, the woman dials her small silver phone, whispers, *Madonna save us*.

A few stay in the room; either they didn't do it or they live here; I hadn't thought of someone living here. One well-dressed man stops, calmly checks the body on the carpet.

"E morto!" he states as if saying the weather is fine.

The stoned woman with burnt hair takes the staple gun.

My cousin says, "They called the police. Let's go, okay?"

"What about an ambulance?"

"Someone said polizia. We have to leave."

"My beer."

"Forget your fucking beer!"

I grab the tiny bag of coke and step over the stained carpet and body in the liminal doorway. Why did I ever walk up this narrow hall? Morto, blood flees the body so quickly and all of us drain the rooms so quickly and down the crowded stairs, slim bodies draped in black suits and pants, knees and arms moving jerkily in black crow angles against sharp white stucco, stucco where you cut your elbow if you touch the wall.

On the street we run past the World War Two tanks again, run like pale ghosts past the Chinese factory and canal water and a distant figure throwing something, a tiny splash in the silver canal, perhaps a stolen phone or the knife.

Men in soccer shirts outside a social club watch my cousin and me come up the sidewalk. They can't know anything. We try to stay calm.

"Scusi," says my cousin. "Train? Trena? Stazione?" Her Italian is better than mine.

They point down the boulevard toward the sea. "Giri a sinistra."

"Left," I say. I know that sinister means left. The left hand is unlucky.

"Si. Sinistra. Andate avanti per due minuti."

"Grazie," says my cousin, "grazie."

"First you come drink with us," the man says.

"Sorry, we must go."

"One drink! To life!"

"Numero di telefono?" another asks hopefully.

"No, no," says my pretty cousin, "I have no phone."

"Sieta a piedi?"

"Si, we're walking."

They grab her ass. "If that was my wife...."

"That's my ass!" I yell. Why did I say that?

"Fuck off," she yells.

"To life!" they yell, I think that's what they yell.

We're walking, now we're running, we run blocks to the train station and I'm gasping; I can ride a bike all day, but I'm not used to running. The station ticket window is empty, no-one there, which is fine by me. I've been travelling on an expired pass that also allows one into art galleries and museums around Napoli. I'll pay a fine, I'm just glad to be on board. Now if we will just move. I can't sit. *Move, move.*

I don't care where the train goes, I just don't want to be around if the polizia are looking for witnesses or a scapegoat, don't want to be a person of interest. Our art school is not officially recognized in Italy.

"Are we supposed to carry our passports? Mine's at the hotel."

"Any blood on us?"

"No-one knows we were there."

We check our clothes for blood splatters anyway, check the bottom of our shoes. Did I walk through the dead man's blood? And that blood sodden tea towel.

"Maybe the guy's ok."

"I'd say he was pretty well gone." Gone west. We sit for what seems like humming hours, then our train betrays that buzzy feeling just before movement begins, that pre-coital imminence, and we sail forward in a silent sway of deliverance.

I remember a funeral for a good friend on the west coast, a lively giant of a man, very well liked. I've never heard so many people say, *He was my best friend.* At the open coffin funeral we sat in solemn pews waiting for the sad service to start and instead the Steppenwolf song *Born to be Wild* roared to life, loud as hell.

Everyone in the chapel laughed; he would have liked that; he laughed a lot. But I saw his big face blank in the coffin and thought yes, he is spent, he is dead, missing. Some force that was him is no longer there (Elvis has left the apartment building). Maybe that's why they have open casket funerals or a wake with the body right in your parlour, so you *know*, really feel the knowledge physically and don't wait for him to show up at your door or expect to see your old friend for a pint in Swan's pub. E morto. You must know.

Our night train will swallow us, will travel all the way to Sorrento. The swallows return. Now, is that Sorrento or Capistrano? A leg with a knife severing a major artery. No more stoned young women for the neighbour with the staple gun. The dead hand, like the men groping women on the subway, *mortua manus*. See the wonders of the ancient world!

"Did you even see who stabbed him?"

"No, no, I just saw legs and a blade swinging." All that blood that should stay inside.

"I just want to be back at the hotel. Be back in Texas."

"We'll be back soon enough."

I show my cousin the stolen baggy.

"You took that from the dead guy? Why?"

"I had some years ago and really liked it, but I could never afford it."

"Fuck, what if we get stopped?"

"I'll get rid of it."

"They'd see you tossing it."

"I don't know. I want to keep it, I want to try some again."

The familiar seats will deliver us back to chapels and chipped frescos and Faberge eggs and our whining art group. The aged conductor on the train so calm in the heat and sweat of day and the ennui of night. Our conductor possesses natural dignity. He does not bring up the idea of tickets. I am glad he runs the train. His childhood bride waits at home; this I am sure of. She is plumper than when they met at the dance and the world was shot in black and white.

The calm conductor and his bride make me think more about marriage. Marriage is success, marriage is failure, marriage is music, a ride, marriage is a train with windows. Every job is a train with windows, everything in the world is a train with windows.

The question is, Do you kick out the windows or do you sit politely and hope for the uniformed conductor? Does our conductor live with his wife in the city of Naples or out in a suburb under the volcano?

A man on the train answers his phone: "Pronto!?" His voice sounds so hopeful. The dead man went pale as we watched. In the mountain tunnels this time no-one kicks out the glass. There is no one Italy, there is a collection of Italys, but this Italy is sombre, in black, this Italy is sixteen coaches long, our train moving beside the sea, on top of the sea, dories on painters bobbing between the stars, white moving lights and the words of the sea, the church, City Hall.

Ah, I recognize where we are now. I'm becoming an old hand, an expert.

Prossima fermata, I say very slowly to my cousin, my best sing-song Italian accent, drawing out the pleasing words as I try them. "Next stop is ours. How are you doing?"

"Rock and roll," she says weakly.

We stop and start, lean into each other, her head fitting under my jaw. I like my cousin's warm form against me.

Eve lies on my hotel bed stripped down to a T-shirt and small white panties. She says, "You don't need to sleep on the floor because of me. But I'm afraid to go to my room. You still have the dead guy's dope?"

"You don't want that now."

Her clean leg by my eye. She says we can share the bed. The unstabbed skin of my cousin's fine thigh leading my eye up to her hips and her secrets, where I want to touch, the tension vibrating in the air like silver wires, I will explode if I don't touch, but I don't touch her. *Mortua manus*, the dead hand. She is restless, but there is no knife in her leg.

"At the topless beach today I was so happy," Eve whispers as she drops into sleep. "I met those Italian boys. We'll pray for him. In a real church. That one with the amazing Caravaggio. Promise?" She is drifting off in my bed and I stay on the sea-coloured tiles the Croatian woman cleans every morning.

Yes, I promise. In my head for some reason an old Blondie tune, *Fade Away and Radiate*; those NYC junkies, how do they hang on? My cousin's face looked so pale reflected in the train window, inside tunnels, inside a dark mountain as if something pushed into a body.

Later that week I see that my souvenir of Naples is gone, my baggy with the dead guy's cocaine is gone. Maybe Naples is also gone, buried once more by the volcano.

Could my cousin taken the baggy? Certainly not clean living Tamika or the conductor who loves his wife. The pretty Croatian woman who cleans my room? Or did I consume all the stolen cocaine during a deranged night and also consume the memory? That has happened before.

Around this same time our aged Director misplaces his fat envelope full of so many Euro notes and now our group is bereft, now we are bankrupt. Is our Dauphin getting dotty or was the cash nicked by the rooftop cat-burglar who plucked an American's Rolex and camera from an open third floor window? The hand coming in the liminal space.

Our director wears a hound's-tooth jacket draped upon his shoulders like a cape, hoping for that continental La Dolce Vita matador look. How will we survive when he has lost all our money? How to pay for meals, for months at the hotel? How will we get home? Perhaps our future holds a giant dine & dash with luggage. Can we sneak our backpacks past the grumpy French woman who never leaves the front desk?

And what happens after you feel the sly knife penetrate your thigh and you die in a kitchen across the hall from your home? Can you bring a staple-gun to heaven? His daughter was there at the party, saw her father die. I don't know how I missed that, but my cousin says it was so. In the hall the weeping daughter held her father in her arms as we left, as he left the country.

The stoned girl with the volcanic hair: I threw my drink on her to help her, I feel we had some link, some strange chemistry. So many things you will never know, so many naked legs you will never touch. But if you do make it to heaven, these matters may seem less important.

Some nights she can't sleep and takes tiny blue pills; my pretty cousin says she remembers the knife, like me she remembers waiting on a train and willing the monster to move. But time passes and we forget. I love time. Time gives me everything, time cracks me up, time kills me.

My wife is from Florida and is moving out of my house while I am in Italy. She takes the dog down to the river and hits a ball into the water with a tennis racket. The moving van comes and the moving van goes. The faithful dog swims to retrieve the ball again and again. Again and again I climb the stairs to my room to pack my bags.

The city in ruins seems to go on forever. Pompeii is so many worlds, so many levels, a strange village below, families caught like an underground zoo, mothers and children frozen in their poses, then a breathing world built just above their heads, busy footsteps on the dead's ceiling, roads and tracks and our slum train's noisy motion just one level above the digs, above their heads, wheels and engines rolling over graves.

It must be odd to live in Pompeii right now and have this shadow city below and to one side, this destroyed duplicate in the basement. Like Las Vegas, like New Orleans, no visitor cares a whit about the real city. In Pompeii we want the roofless ruins, those ancient bedrooms and brothels and shops broken open to the sun. The excavations are fantastic, but locals must resent this favoured twin, this magnet shadow so close to them.

And we are the same, that other place shadowing us here, the lost place we left and must return to, return to a face and cheques to be written at the kitchen table and deep leaves to be raked past the backyard swing, a return to winter and shovelling a driveway and a new battery and heavy duty wipers, a return to providing and caring and staying put. Will that cooler world stay put while I am gone from it?

Outside under the latest model of the sun I try to stay in shade, creep close to a building, veer under pine trees and cypress. Pack on my back, I walk to the ruins, excavations at my feet, dead conversations with that woman in Canada in my head.

Did I say I am fascinated by Pliny and his demise in Pompeii? I travelled to Pompeii because of Vesuvius the volcano and the excavated ruins, but also because Pliny sailed there. In Pompeii the sky grew dark after the eruption and the sun stood still under the volcano.

On a morning just like this the volcano woke over the vineyards and all of this city was buried deep, left to sleep so long; amphitheatre and villas and cobbled lanes and cowering families covered over. Children and babies hold each other and suffocate in seconds, then discovered by chance, dug out and exposed once more to the harsh sun and to tourists like me, the sun inching forward a crimson ribbon at a time, their ancient roof peeled back and the living come to visit the long sunlit avenues of the dead.

26

At the station I bump into Ray Ray and Tamika from our group in Rome. As we chat on an outdoor platform, a high-speed train pulls in for a brief stop.

A stray Jack Russell terrier trots around full of pep, the stray dog wants to cross the tracks from our platform to see who is at the station, but the streamlined train blocks the dog's path. The diesel will leave any second, we know; these high speed trains never stop for long. The little dog peers this way and that for a way to cross the track. The dog places his head between wheels of the idling train. We all groan when he does this.

"Don't."

We see his quick terrier eyes and brain working in tandem: *Can I sneak through the iron wheels?* The crowd tenses as if the curious dog awaits a guillotine, the lull between beheadings.

"No," I say out loud, "come back." But the dog does not know English. Tamika turns away, she can't watch.

"Here!" The dog turns, runs back to our platform, the train shrieks and wheels scythe where his head had been a moment before.

"Good boy!" He has bright eyes and soft brown ears. I saved him, I am Pliny the Elder. I must have a treat in my backpack. It's a Jack; it doesn't want to be petted; it wants to run, it wants to run until it dies. I know this dog will die. It has no-one.

Tamika and Ray Ray ask me to hike with them up the slopes of the volcano. Only days, weeks ago, Ray Ray hung out in the Hong Kong meatpacking district; he tells us of suitcases full of gifts in China.

"Shoes, electronics, they cost nothing there! The Customs people wouldn't believe me when I declared the total value, they thought I was lying. They held me for hours."

For hours we climb the side of the volcano, sweating like mules in the sun and rock, the drugging sun. In the scrub brush we halt, knowing we're not going to make the peak, the Gran Cono. I've seen satellite photos from directly above the cone, this strange opening, this gash, a black hole in the planet. Pliny died doing this, he stopped and didn't get up, covered in ash and molten lava. Shelley burns on the beach, I burn in Pompeii. My scalp is toast, my head hurting.

Below the mountain African men sell new sunglasses to an ancient nation; the tall men set up tiny tables on street or a cloth spread on the sidewalk outside the church. Southern Italy so warm, a boot aimed at Africa, a long fashionable boot, so close to Tunisia, to Cleopatra's Egypt and golden breast, artifacts taken from Nubian locales scattered everywhere in Italy. North Africa was part of Caesar's empire, and Mussolini's empire, Africa is so close, yet black people seem like strangers in the living-room.

"Italians treat you like family," says Father Kelly at the restaurant. "Italians are wonderful, so warm."

This is not always so for African street vendors or those in our group with darker skin like Tamika from Philly or Ray Ray from Nigeria. My old uncle used to say, We are made of the same dough, but we are baked in different ovens.

In a café a woman beside me is talking of money. Is this what it seems? Non ho capito, my Italian is very poor, I lack language, the secret code.

Thirty Euro, thirty pieces of silver. The possibility should not be a surprise. A few blocks from our table are frescos of Roman orgies and ancient delights, and shop entrances boasted their good luck charms of erect penises, and pictures of Priapus, the god of gardens and fertility, Priapus proudly weighing his giant cock on a scale, his cock out in front of him like the neck of a goose.

A few blocks away in the ruins are faded frescos of cunnilingus. But what if I am misunderstanding her? Is that her man there at the curb? I could be beaten or killed over an insult, over a woman's honour.

The woman with curly hair speaks to me again. It sounds like quindici, or is it dieci? Fifteen, or perhaps ten, or is it nineteen? Why would she say an odd number like nineteen? I wish I knew for sure what was happening. She seems to be bargaining, dropping the price rapidly. Did she take "For you" as a ploy, an insult? I don't want to insult anyone, I just arrived, I want to wait a few days before insulting anyone.

No, I say, No, grazie. I say it several times, trying to be polite, that I am grateful for something, her attention, not wanting to insult her. Grazie.

Across the bay at the naval base at Misenum, Pliny the Elder saw the massive cloud the shape of a tree. Pliny took swift galleys to Pompeii to help old friends stranded on the shore of the bay, to help them escape. He died near this spot, a hero, gave himself right here.

The café woman walks away from me, walks away looking hard at her phone, leaning forward toward the square eye of the screen. Her eyes are changed, her face no longer friendly. I've seen that look before, that sea change.

A man sits down to show me his mangled hands, a refugee from Tunisia, he crossed the desert then he floated in a boat to the island of Lampedusa. In Italy he has tried to remove his own fingerprints, he has burnt his hands, afraid the police will send him back. They have his fingerprints registered.

Will I give him five Euro?

No.

I no longer want my place at the table, I want to walk too, a street walker, I walk the city, walk and turn into an alley as a shortcut to the basilica and central piazza. I think I know my direction, my landmarks, but the alley turns the wrong way, turns away from the centre and keeps going and going and I'm alone and start to get jumpy, paranoid, I've made a bad move, entered a box canyon. This encounter with this woman and then the man with the burnt hands, this has thrown me, I was so happy to arrive here, but I am edgy now walking around waiting for lurking strumpets and robbers to jump me. Perhaps the guidebook is right about Pompeii: the world is full of foul deeds and sneaking mischief, a mousetrap, miching mallecho, a cold beer and a knife between the ribs.

All around the bay the Nuvoletta-Polverino cartels open suit-cases and sell groceries, garlic, and leather, hash and high fashion gowns, ecstasy and cocaine in the northern suburbs, stolen antiquities and jewels in the narrow lanes and the train moves past ruins, a uniformed man calling for tickets, tickets. And yet I ride the train for free most days, my pass expired, a Unico Campania Three Day Travel Ticket. I am rarely asked, trusted or I am invisible, of a certain age, so no-one checks my fingerprints to see if I should be deported. I don't have to burn my hands.

Circumvesuviana, the local train circles the mountain, the violent mountain held over us no matter where we go until I feel it has always been there, looming over me all my life. The ancient vineyards rise in long perfect lines to the volcano, a series of triangles and convergences and my eye follows eagerly, pleased by the sightline.

The area around the Bay of Naples is so fertile, crops in sun and soil enriched by the repeated ash eruptions, grapes and arbours and orchards and flowers, and all this beautiful coastline, this sea stretching away in the sun, all these islands, all this potential, so I wonder: Why does it seem so fucked up? Grapes and blossoms, but also trash piled in cul de sacs and vandalism and graffiti like ugly tattoos and larceny and no work and graft and gangs and payoffs and homicide. In suburbs of Naples men cut packages into vials, kilos roll in and the kilos roll out. And the money? Where does it go? Like water, it has to go somewhere.

Ray Ray and Tamika catch a milk train to Sorrento, but I travel the other way to a smaller excavation site. Coming back I find a seat in a compartment with two men and an elderly woman. Two seats left. I sense each passenger's unspoken hope that no-one else comes into our compartment. Then a young woman struggling with a heavy case. I jump up and I help lift her suitcase up on the high rack above our seats.

She sits beside me, flushed in the face from exertion and heat, introduces herself. Abby, an American, she has been teaching in Istanbul, but her contract is done.

I'd love to see Istanbul, I say.

She is travelling for a month and will meet her parents in Venice; next year she will teach in Asia. She asks if I can translate a sign for her.

The older man in our compartment says, You come to Italy and can't speak Italian? He has a dark upswept pompadour and leans forward, head deep between his shoulders, like Elvis with osteoporosis.

So all travellers must speak his language? Then how would I ever see Russia or China?

30

You must be very careful in Napoli, he says to Abby.

He points to his eyes. At first I thought he meant they'll go for your eyes, but then I realize he is demonstrating that he has seen of what he speaks with his own eyes.

"This is not a normal country. Here up is down, down is up. Here everyone wants a share off the top and a share off the bottom and a share off the side and then what is left? Since the war? A new government every nine months, as if having a baby. But what is the result? When the Americani voted for that fool Bush I laughed. But now we have elected a buffone, a clown. Now I can't laugh. And the criminals. Even the football matches are fixed, it's all contaminated. In the old days Mussolini would take care of them. If you stepped out of line back then, this is what happened to you." He makes a motion of slitting his own throat.

I have my hand on her neck, it seems so intimate. Abby and I walk the Naples train station together. *Attenzione Ai Borseggiatori*—Beware of Pickpocket! We sit for a drink at the station. Vore una birra, per favore. Vore many beer, per favore. She asks me if I have been to the Gaspé; she went as a child and still remembers.

Yes, it's beautiful, gannets and whales and so much light. Her head is there and I can see down her top and spy what is hidden, her black bra and small breasts nestled there. I am allowed to touch her shoulders and neck. Yes, the Gaspé is beautiful.

I know it's impossible, but I want to skip the awkward courtship steps, the phone calls, restaurant candles watching scallops shuck their bacon wraps. Can't we simply look at each other once and know and walk by the sea and lie down. Can't I just say, *You and me*. And we would both somehow know it's right.

"E-mail me," I say to Abby, worried about cementing things before I leave for Pompeii. "I'll check at the internet café."

"No need to check, I'll see you in Pompeii soon."

When she says this to me I adore our world. Abby walks into Naples and I take another slow train south, the right side unspooling views of the aqua sea and up lift the tribal cameras and always a church up like a narrow knife, the body heat increasing markedly inside the cars as the train travels along the bay to

31

Pompeii. Canada's snow or ice seems impossible in this drugging heat.

In train tunnels we travel in and out of light, in an out of mountains, pupils dilating, pores sweating. In Pompeii's raw ruins I enter another tunnel on foot, down into the forum, the amphitheatre, this place where they died. A dark passage leads down at an angle, into the ground, I follow the tunnel to get out of the relentless sun and down into the lower level of the forum, the Teatro, down into shade, hiding from the sun, even for a few rare moments.

Tamika and Ray Ray spot me from afar; they cross the dust and pigeons and follow me into the underworld. The dark tunnel passage is cool, shade is so lovely, so good to be briefly out of the sun under the forum complex; the burnt skin of my forehead hurts so much it worries me.

They found a horse when digging under this forum, torches once burned in these haunted underground halls, animals and men waiting, waiting, sweating, then your turn, it's time, pushed out into the harsh sun, live or die.

From the level forum floor we raise our eyes to the rising rows of stone seats heaped above us.

"I suspect this was a very bad view for most who saw it."

The majority of people would be above looking down. This minority on the floor of the forum standing where we stand breathing at the bright bottom of the stone walls—slaves, foreign exiles, prisoners of war, gladiators, *infamia* pushed out into the sun—well, in a few moments most would be killed.

Trident pitchforks to the skull, Roman stabbing swords, curved Bulgarian swords, chains and nets and shields, starved African lions with their ribs showing and a chanting mob overhead (do you feel lucky, punk) and, at the end, dragged bleeding across the sand by Juno in his mask, dragged behind the walls by masked Juno who swings his square hammer into the private curve of your porcelain head.

In the ruins I see a dog running and jumping in the distance. The dog runs over lava and candy wrappers and king's tombs.

It's the same Jack Russell terrier I saw at the train station with its head in the diesel's wheels. In this heat the crazy dog chases pigeons in the grassy ruins of the Grande Palace, the dog galloping by ancient Corinthian pillars lined up in rows, pillars or stumps left to hint of the space where emperors and nobles roamed vast gardens and pools.

The running dog cares not a whit about gardens or hidden history or the future or the heat, the dog cares only for the moment and the nearest pigeon. The dog is running full speed in the heat when I arrive and is running full speed when I leave. Its pink tongue hangs and I hear the creature pant, a clicking sound.

"How does a dog find water here?" The sandy ground is like a desert.

The terrier turns to me and speaks with its beautiful brown eyes: Yes, I am the same dog you saw at the railroad track. I appreciate your concern, but you can do nothing for me. You are visiting here briefly, a stranger, a foreigner, while this is my life, short as it may be. You are used to one way, I am used to another.

An Irish boy jumps away nervously as the dog madly rockets past running down a pigeon he will never catch. The dog turns and runs again, over and over. That woman in Canada, I must change her mind, I must swim with her again.

And I must tell my cousin Eve of the dog; she'd understand, Eve is my new confessor. Does the dog bark at Italian pigeons in Italian? It has no owner. The terrier is a stranger. The terrier is me.

We stagger in the heat, we must leave the dog, leave these ruins for a drink, leave this skin that feels so sore from the merciless sun. We tromp the same Italian dust that slaves and emperors and gladiators ate. Place this ancient soil in your mouth like a thick piece of pizza pie. Eat the rich past. Dig in the ground anywhere in Italy and you find the past, you can't escape your past.

In the family hotel the staff and family members eat after we have been fed and our plates cleared. The mother with dyed blond hair and the tired father with his neck brace—once so handsome in the old black and white photos decorating the lobby and halls, posing with movie stars and soccer players, but now he spends the day in the lobby with a tiny TV set and a neck brace. Now they are aged parents, watching Euro Cup on a tiny TV.

Big Pico, my favourite waiter, sits with the family, and beside him sits a skinny cook; they lean together at the same table in mid-afternoon, huge man and thin man leaning toward each other over delicious plates and much wine. This is their time, not ours, an intimate inner circle, relaxed and pleasantly tired from waiting on us, serving the guests breakfast and lunch.

The German man in the café says to me, Italians all lie, they promise you something and don't deliver, they laze about, nothing on time or when promised. I'll never come back, he says. A horrible place.

He hates it here, yet I love it so, the same place. I love Italy.

The German claims that southern Italians are lazy, but Pico in Pompeii works so very hard for us. My hotel room has no clock and I travel light, no watch, no cell-phone, no laptop. My glazed window does not reveal if it is 5 AM or 9 AM. So down to the lobby to spy a clock, and I glimpse Pico bent in the kitchen creating his raw pastry, no-one else about at this hour. He is here at dawn, he is here at night: when does he live, when does he sleep? I worry whether he has a life outside this hotel, whether he is lonely, whether will die from work. He is not lazy.

After another luscious dinner at the hotel, Pico brings me a simple repast, a lone superb pear with a knife and fork.

Okay? Pico asks me.

Si, si!

Did he read my mind? The single pear is exactly what I need after all these rich dishes, such beautiful texture and sweet taste.

Prego, Pico says so kindly every night, his hand and arm out like a silent film actor directing me to my lonely table, welcoming me to the table for one, the one solitary place setting among the hotel's couples and families and singing nuns. I am in my place.

Abby, the woman from the train, said she'd meet me here today at four or she'd call the hotel. The phone rings at the front desk;

34

I strain to listen. Is it her? No call, no email. The sirens do not call to me from the blue grotto.

The dog runs past. I sit outside the hotel at a wobbly wicker table with a huge cold bottle (*grande per favore*), waiting for her. I keep buying more big bottles in the lobby and the old man does not approve.

Trying to seduce a young American woman on the train to Naples is somehow more honourable than paying a prostitute in Pompeii. Where lies the logic? We were walking and kissing after the train, strangers on a train; I was allowed a view under her blouse, but I will never quite get under that enticing black bra. She decides I must wait.

I can't live like this much longer. I thought she'd make me whole somehow, keep the pieces together, would be my duct tape. All these people in the street, at the store: how do they do it? They move directly, they know what they want! They function as if they designed themselves and no need for duct tape.

"What's up, fool?" Ray Ray and Tamika join me at my table.

"Look what the cat dragged in. Pull up a chair." I buy them anything they want, happy to see them, to break my funk, my lowered mood, happy to have company at my lonely table in Fortress Europe.

Stucco walls line the road. A yellow sky smeared like oil-paint and above that yellow streak perches a dark mumbling thunderstorm. No rain in weeks and now we drink in a giant jagged tunnel, light waning after a bright boiling day. The new weather alters the air's colour, the street in front of the hotel moves many shades of mauve, and finally it rains, canary-coloured plaster darkens in rain, welcome rain.

Thunder and lightning reverberate over the ruins of Pompeii; our nervous hotel dog opens his jaws and speaks to the sparking sky, loose dogs loping everywhere. We sit in wicker chairs and watch the sky and the street and the dogs.

The wild dogs running free make Tamika jumpy. We walk to the central piazza and dogs trot out of nowhere, surrounding us while we look for a bank machine.

"Damn! That's not right!" she exclaims, looking all around.

"Where are they coming from? I don't like them running free."

Ray Ray stops to talk with any other blacks he sees in Italy. He grabs my arm, asks me, "Where is *nowhere?*"

"What do you mean?"

"Those guys I just talked to say they live in nowhere."

"They're homeless? They live on the street?"

"No! A real place, man, they said they live in nowhere."

A place called nowhere; I have to think about this one.

"It's way up north, man, they said it's a good place, I should come visit."

"It's a country up north?"

"Yeah, man, way up there."

"Norway?"

"Yes, man! Nowhere! It's a good place. I should go up and see Nowhere, I don't dig it here in Italy." He lowers his voice. "In fact, I think I'll leave tomorrow," Ray Ray tells me in a confidential tone.

"Give it a chance."

"Man, they liked me way more in China. They bow to you! In China they treated me like a king. They don't like me here in Italy."

In Italy we walk such crowded cities and underground grottos stuffed with grinning skeletons crowded in bunks and deep hallways like mineshafts and then on trains I see so much empty countryside between the cities. Millions crammed close into projects and slums and yet so much wide open country just out the door, just down the road. The same is true in Canada, the same all around the world.

We don't want lebensraum, we shun the orchard above the stream. No, we love cement curbs and peeling walls, if we are not born inside the city we move there as soon as we can, we follow our bliss, our desire for hustle and excitement and dumpsters and rats in stairwells and staple-guns and opiates, to hang out on a concrete corner or line up for a bonehead job and pick each other's pocket and scent doorways with the ammonia of our urine and exist without leafy trees or pink blossoms, our desire to avoid God and nature, to take elevators, to ride machines climbing toward boxes set atop boxes like bone ossuaries set in the sky, our manic desire to stand on each other's head to the soundtrack of machines on the walls and machines past the window circling the sky and machines rumbling the ground under our feet.

Ray Ray said yesterday that he felt sick; maybe he caught something in China.

I ask, "How you doing today?" I shouldn't have said that they spit in our food.

"Man, thank you for asking. I could be dying and that dude running this show doesn't care." Ray Ray says, "I've had it, man, I'm leaving tomorrow." He says this to me every day.

All the trains in the gloaming and buses beneath olive valleys and aqueducts and trefoil arches in plumes of diesel. Our group always on the move like vapour, up and down, back and forth over roses and skeletons, changing towns and minds, changing trains and tunnels, crowded platforms and subterranean stairs and no seats on the trains and such sweaty carriages under the looming volcano and cactus and lava fields and burning rock once taken for portals to hell.

A shantytown burns below a freeway (is it a Roma enclave?) and I know I could drip my endless sweat over the class-war conflagration and easily extinguish the flames. I have never sweated like this, I'm sure our collective sweat will pool on the floor of the train until our ankles are deep in sweat, in aqua vitae, the saltwater of life.

The city streets at night—ah I can still conjure the scent of crazed Vespas in the heaped garbage and brilliantined pickpockets—then to pull ourselves from a mattress at dawn for another woozy train to Pompeii's sun-bright ruin, and a milk-train back again to Naples in sore shoes to climb a narrow thirteenth-century alley of cobbles and scooters and skewback abutments and we dodge the Vespas and wolf down the best food ever laid against my tongue.

The Napoli station, where I last saw Abby, makes me feel like a loser, the Napoli station a sad axis. I buy a ticket at a machine. All the redolent names, Pompeii, Herculaneum, Sorrento,

Amalfi, Positano, and soon we will be back in the bosom of peach-coloured Rome.

We climb on the last train and down the aisle. I take a seat on the right. Ray Ray takes a seat on the left of the aisle. Ray Ray tells me he is the second son of second wife, he says this is lower status than the eldest son. This was years back in Nigeria. I never know what to believe, what is real.

Ray Ray says to me, "Bet you five Euro no-one will sit by me."

I've gotten to know Ray Ray in Italy; he chases all the Croatian chambermaids and is a bit of a con man, but he is a creampuff at heart; at a party he worried I hadn't eaten and deftly cooked me a seafood stir-fry. But he is so tall and black; the Italians fear him.

"Will you take my bet?" Ray Ray asks me. "Five Euro."

Sure, why not. Someone will sit by him. The seats around me fill up. The rest of the train fills. The feeling of pure will as the train shunts out of the station, every seat taken except for three blue seats around Ray Ray.

To my surprise, Rome's rouge walls seem calmly familiar and pleasing to the eye after Napoli's grey forms and volcanic dust and volcanic drugs and jackal bedlam and mountains of aromatic refuse and a knife steering its calm way through the air of a kitchen party. Naples is more compelling, stranger and wilder than Rome, a fascinating paella, the true capital of Italy, but now as I walk Rome it seems almost a home, as if I know it well and have spent some worthy part of my life here, which may not be true, but is a comforting feeling since I seem to have lost my sense of home.

We leave the train station and subway and stumble up into ground level sunlight and a tiny corridor of mirrors that passes for a hotel lobby, so many puzzled versions of me. This narrow hallway seemed lunatic the first time I saw it and now seems so normal. The French woman at the desk hasn't moved all her life and sends me to my same room, the same terrace waiting at the top of the same stairs, which pleases me. See, I am not always morbid. It's as if the French woman and the American intern kept the room empty just for me.

My cousin Eve finds me for a drink and chat on my high terrace. I'm living near the top of a tree; I stare out at Rome and the green parrot in the tall trees pleases me; trees sway in green hours and I water my flowers again. They survived my absence. No sign of the smoking Spanish woman in the atrium, but my orphans and nuns below make me happy.

My cousin agrees. "It's so beautiful here; it makes me happy. That sun every morning. Italy makes me happy. But I have trouble with happiness; I'm suspicious of it. My mother always said I was a very serious child. I should eat something. You're always laughing at me, mocking me."

"I am not mocking you." (I am more mocked than mocking.)

A light dusting of freckles on my cousin's lovely skin, like an animal imprint. I like them. She hates the freckles, uses lemon juice to fade them. My cousin tells me she has had two periods in one month. Short cycles, she says, and lots of blood. One day I saw her wince from a cramp and gave her some of my painkillers. She washes her sheets in her shower and dries them on my terrace, which has more room and sun. I give her raisins for iron, give her a cold German beer. "Did you know," she says, "that the beer bottle was invented in 1850?"

"I did not know that." We drink, eat apples from Afghanistan, dates from the Euphrates.

At the café at night she orders a dish called strangled priests and observes that I am like her mother putting butter on everything. It is odd to consider how much butter have I swallowed in my life, how many gallons, barrels, trucks, ocean-going tankers.

My cousin Eve tells us of the time she entered a tiny taverna deep in the south of Italy, asked a man for directions and an ancient woman spit on my cousin's bare arm.

"She spit on you for real?" asks Ray Ray.

My cousin says amiably, "I was wearing a top that showed too much skin."

Usually she carried two shawls: one for her shoulders and one for her head, in case she was going into a church or formal event, but she didn't think she needed a shawl in this shop.

"Man, no-one spit on me in China," says Ray Ray. "Seriously."

We eat and drink and walk and I realize I missed the streets and lovely murky rivers to the sea, what is borne by the chartered river past the red palaces, the peach-coloured walls and cheetah shadows and forlorn Italian faces and frank sexual fashions. And I missed my cousin. I tell her of the angry prostitute in Pompeii and of Abbey's no-show.

She says, You are such a fool with women, but she laughs at my tales.

On my terrace I stand and survey my kingdoms, my holy Roman empires, another Pope, a new King of Rome! I am a spy in a tower and who are these statues I spy? If I stand on a chair on my terrace and look several blocks east I can see a glass and brass cupola and a group of polished white statues in situ on one corner of a building high above the huge Vatican walls.

My statues are not near the giant violet Basilica, they are far from the centres of power; my statues inhabit a lost corner above the Vatican's north wall, isolated in some plaintive ex-Catholic exile, their perch high with the birds and helicopters.

Perhaps the statues are from the list of murdered Popes, or pretenders or disbarred lawyers or weird patron saints, set off on their own cliff edge.

Here is the odd thing: I search the street directly under the wall, but I can never spot this mysterious group from below. I zigzag my neighbourhood crossroads and avenues, and follow the huge wall, which should lead me right to them, but there is never any sight of them. My statues only exist when I see them from my rooftop terrace, they are simply not visible from ground level. Am I the only one who sees them? Look, there they are, looking out over the city, but if I run down the stairs they do not exist.

I become more and more fascinated by this lonely lovely group of statues. They seem thuggish, hip. Why can I not find them? Do I need to sneak inside the Vatican walls? The Mexican rock climber from our group went over the wall for a lark and was caught by the Pope's Swiss Guard and put on the next flight to Mexico and the rest of us were nearly kicked out of the country.

My cousin and others in the group make a day trip to the beach at Ostia. Such heat, not used to it, air wavering in heat, like fumes dancing over a nozzle at a gas pump. My cousin's sun-burnt shoulders are so red and tender, and in the evening we are altered, groggy, as if felled by sunstroke, *coup de soleil*.

I have a round plastic container from the discount store, sooth-ing cold cream, Crema Corpo, for her tender shoulders. She opens her blouse in my hotel room. It's better if I don't know such things, if I am not allowed to see.

In the amazing ruins we eat apples, in the amazing ruins of the temples, of marriage. There stands my cousin and her legs and lingering glances. Do not go near there, do not follow her frock in the frescoes as wild dogs run past, *mondo cane*, a dog's world.

Man is his dizzy desire and I desire knowledge of her bare shoulders, that curved planet, that new home. Her neck part of a naked crescent, a lovely curve from naked earlobe to naked shoulder. Why do I love her neck so, that nexus of delicate ear and fine hair and shampoo scent, the shoulders, the skin, the jaw and cheek, the shadows and perfume; it has everything, right there. I can hide my face there; what a world exists just there!

She asks for lotion for her skin. I approach my cousin with a round container of lotion from an Italian shop, approach a planet, once distant, now in view in Rome, a room with a view. Her shoulders glow in the spacecraft window, closer, closer to touch, a new looming planet, the lightest touch, my fingers like landing craft and her intake of breath.

Crema Corpo, Revitalizzanta Aloe Vera. Rubbing her tender shoulders and her neck, her back, lightly down her spine to her round hips. I worry she'll get mad, but I can feel her body move nicely to my touch. She stretches her neck and shoulders, mur-muring pleasant sounds, moves into my pressure as a cat will.

I will not lie with her, but I keep rubbing more lotion, her shoulders and back and lower and lower down her back, on the sides of her hips and brief forays near her belly and a bit lower below her navel, teasing, testing, lower and lower, circling closer and closer, so close, but never all the way.

My cousin says, "You have such a calming effect on me."

"Me?" My mind is always racing and my life is chaos.

"You seem very calm." An East German woman travelling in the west of Ireland said the same thing to me, used a German word for calm.

My hands wander, my mind wanders, catacombs and tunnels and travel, planes, airports and tunnels, my mind inside her, the lines where her strap was in the sun, the lines and borders, the line and colour of her face, the lineament of her eye and cheekbone skin. I think of the old woman in the south of this country spitting on Eve's skin. Country matters.

My cousin gasps when my fingers stray and find where she is wet, my fingers connect with her brain, a direct tendril, another hidden passageway, her breath quiet as the mountain town that makes you sing.

My hand wrecked a marriage, wrecked unions, and I killed the beautiful scooter couple, and I listen to the Fleshtones, their best album, *Roman Gods*. At night when I get under the covers my cousin seems awake, but she mutters a language I can't understand.

What did you say?

She kicks my shin or calf. Is she being impish? She pulls at my hair. How to interpret this? She goes back to sleep, breathing rhythmically.

The next day she laughs with joy at my account. I kicked you? I spoke gibberish? She recalls none of it. She leaves my room like a sleepwalker. Soon we will all leave Rome. We move, we sin, we confess, we fly to and fro, we are on earth, then we are in the heavens, then we are not, we are on earth, then we are flung through the heavens, then we are not in the heavens.

And she loves me, then she loves me not, she becomes another woman who says in a doorway or in an airport, says I'd hate to lose touch with you, you know I love you in so many ways. Another one who says, It's been wonderful, as did Natasha, Natasha my buried past, another quiet buried city.

"Don't be depressed," my cousin says, "I know you'll be depressed." Or did Natasha in Canada say that? All these people living in your past as if in a nearby apartment building and waiting for you to get there. The anatomy of desire and the anatomy of loss—I have them mixed up in my depressed, sun-burnt head.

My cousin looks pale in the train window. My cousin is in my room, no, she is gone, she is walking a narrow lane miles away, she is coming downhill in another country, she walks a line between whitewashed homes that have been there forever, a lane curving this way and that and quiet as a suture. She leaves my room, leaves the station, leaves the airport and somewhere a waitress carries a big curved glass just for me.

In Pompeii last week the hunched train lurched forward and the steel wheels did not slice off the dog's head. Perhaps like the dog I'll persist, survive. Perhaps the terrier did hear and heed me, perhaps the terrier knows many languages, will travel to Russia and China, will visit the chambermaids in Croatia. The sunny peak and the valley depth so close together. The scooter couple is so beautiful, yet they die high above the charming sea, the shallow coast, they fall from the ledge, the ledger.

In my last days in Rome I grow obsessed by my group of statues peopling a ledge, I stare out from my terrace and I pace back and forth on blisters under the Vatican's high walls; I must find where they live high above us. I borrow binoculars from the American intern.

As I focus the binocs on the statues they turn their heads to look at me, lean to speak with each other, as if posing for an album cover, say early Blues Magoos or Velvet Underground. One statue wears Bob Dylan sunglasses, resembles Lou Reed. Another pats his perfectly curled hair. They whisper to each other and one statue turns his hips, wags a pale erection at me, his Roman good luck charm, a large statue gripping his generous phallus with two large hands high above the milling streets crowded with tourists all dressed in motley.

We meet in the street and my new gang of ghostly statues brings me along on a mission. They are not murdered Popes, they are not exiled saints. No, their ambitions are far simpler, for they are lard thieves, they steal used grease, fryer oil. The statue with Lou Reed ringlets is the ringleader. We gather in the alley behind the famous restaurant, for money is to be had in rancid lard and biodiesel, the price climbs daily and they know someone who knows someone who can move grease, who takes this filth off our hands.

43

Cats rub our legs in the long alley. Wild cats roam Rome's ancient sunken ruins while dogs run free in Pompeii's train station, and this speaks to something about each city: Rome is feline and Pompeii is canine.

In June my cousin sang songs while we kayaked and her lovely voice carried and she rose from the sea with jellyfish stings like red scratches or burns. Swim into jellyfish and recoil and try to escape their touch, and the next day small red whiplashes on her right shoulder and breast. She put toothpaste on the stings to soothe them. My cousin Eve is afraid to go into the sea again.

My cousin leaves me over and over, on a bicycle, in a kayak, but she comes back over and over, vague as Janus, divided as Janus. I have such faith in the future. I love the future just because it is so nicely vague; the future's so vague I have to wear shades.

In the alley of grease we have our duties. If anyone stops us, my role is to pretend to be a lost tourist and speak English only, though the statues insist to me that police have their hands full with murders and the mob and the ultras and can't be bothered with small transgressions regarding fryer oil. The grease in the alley reeks. Lewd Priapus is with us, but he is not popular, his huge phallus gets in the way of lugging the sloppy plastic drums.

"Clearly he is of little use in enterprises such as these."

Pliny the Elder died rescuing people from the volcano and here I am stealing lard. Pliny was noble, took a fast cutter to the shore. "Fortune goes to the brave!" Pliny shouted into the wind. Now there was a man! I must make some changes in my life.

No, you are wrong, says Priapus beside me in the alley. No, I knew Pliny well and he had grown quite corpulent, he died sitting down and his friends abandoned him in the pumice. He was no admiral, he was given the post as a patronage appointment. He sailed across the bay, but wind pinned his cutter to the shore and there was no rescue so they waited and feasted and drank and slept until the volcano drove them from the dwelling, pillows tied to their heads as helmets. Out on the burning pumice Pliny collapsed, he asked a slave to kill him.

That can't be true, I insist.

44

Yes, he couldn't breathe, he sat down and couldn't stand up and the party was afraid of being covered in ash and lava. His friends left him, left him lying on one of his sails for a bed. They are as bad as we are, sinners all of us.

Near the Vatican a tall American man glares at our procession of pale talking statues dragging big drums of grease. He turns to his wife.

"When we get back home, at church?" His Dockers are creased beautifully, his posture erect; at some point he commanded aircraft carriers in the Pacific.

"Yes, honey?" she says to him.

"I'm not giving another cent."

His wife lingers, her wistful eyes linger on Priapus's dangling gifts. Can this elephant trunk be real? A man lies face down on the sidewalk outside the Vatican walls; he twitches, but he does not look up at the passing crowd, as if the sidewalk is a movie screen he is studying. Are the dark lumps pushing from his scalp sign of a true disease? They look like small wooden knobs, knobs fashioned from dark-grained wood. In Rome we are learning about craft, art, faith. Can we have confidence, can we believe in this affliction of the head?

The swarthy man lies begging face down on a wide sidewalk below the Vatican walls, one of his hands reaching straight out for alms. Tourists are forced to step around his twitching form. They cross the street to join a lineup at the bustling gelato shop, choose gelato the colour of tulips.

Is the man prone on the sidewalk a Gypsy or Roma? A Turk? Croatian? Albanian? We tiptoe around him, around his flat arm, wondering whether the lumps on his head are real or a con job to elicit sympathy and more coins.

Before she left, my cousin lay pale as a statue under my hand, my white body cream spread over her back, and this swarthy man lying on the sidewalk, one arm out to beg, dark as a collier. Doves gather around us like doubts. Have confidence, have faith, believe in the man with his arm outstretched.

We move on to our reward, our cash, we move on with our drums of grease. The statues have a gig tonight playing Fleshtones covers, a cafe near Via Cola di Rienzo; maybe I'll sit in on harmonica, try out my new silver chromatic. The other statues are resentful of Priapus and his weighty phallus, the way he smiles to show it off.

"Last time we bring him along," mutters one.

"He's going to ruin my $50 buzz."

"I get tired of looking at it," adds another.

"Yeah guys, I think I'm gonna jet."

We resent Priapus, yet we have a strange pride in knowing him. You should see this thing! We tell our wives and girlfriends about his gifts, which might be dangerous if they become curious to know more, to become intimately acquainted with such a formidable phallus.

On my terrace I hear splashing sounds and gleeful voices; I peer over the edge. My orphans: in this insane heat someone has given my orphans a wading pool! This makes me very happy. The nuns and orphans will never know that I care, that I watch from above like a powerless God, that I look out and I am happy for them and their little wading pool. We are all playful orphans seeking to splash each other. Our needs are simple.

Now I need to call a taxi. This final steadfast servant arrives the hotel door, the most silent man in Italy, perhaps the only silent man in Italy, and to this driver I gladly hand over my gold and last coins and folded bills of colour, the last of my amusing Euros, and the quiet Italian steers me to the portals of an airport named after the genius Leonardo da Vinci, west of Rome (in my head the suicide Vic Chesnutt sings sadly).

I'm not happy to leave, but I am happy I came, I saw, I want to come back, *vorrei ub biglietto e ritorno. Ritorno*, that sounds so nice, return to the light dusting of freckles on my cousin's lovely skin. Under the volcano she orders a dish called strangled priests, mutters a language I can't understand, kisses me, kicks me. In Napoli or Pompeii, what were they eating, what were they saying, who were they kissing and kicking when the volcano hit and buried them? The coast so beautiful there below the volcano.

Pliny couldn't walk and was buried in ash, they came back to find his body in the cremated world, the buried world, and the beautiful scooter couple dies on the narrow Amalfi coast road, so narrow, a wall to one side and empty sea air on the other side. Such fine views and the musical bus horn like a pleasing trumpet flourish at each corner and tunnel.

Vespa means wasp. The red scooter weaves quickly through cars, streaks through a galaxy of colours, roars inside a brief noisy tunnel and exits the tunnel and in the next sunny curve an oncoming bus strays over the line and a scooter bounces off the non-committal front of the bus and breaks into many pieces, the scooter breaks into one wheel and side mirrors and the bright plastic orbs of signal lights.

The boyfriend's helmet stays on his head, but the young woman's helmet flies away and the crushed scooter and the young woman skids across the road, bare legs, no helmet, the ruin of her dress and skin, and she tumbles past the cliff edge like a scrap from a plate, like luggage tossed from a balcony.

She falls past the cliff turning in air, her legs up behind her and spinning down toward the green sea and her green eyes aim up at the clouds. And the boy sits on the road far above, helmet on like a diver, his suit torn like sausage casing; the injured boy studies his broken legs and lives to know that he killed the girl on his scooter. An idea blooming in his head, quiet as the white towel that once fell from her hip. He crawls toward the edge.

Many Greeks sailed these seas before Christ did, before Christ became a fisher of men, pirate kings ran this coast and invasion fleets waited, nervous men in rows, planes filling a sky overhead with silk. So many voices calling, but the bus driver can't open the bus door, bent by the impact to the front of the bus. We can't get off the bus to stop him.

The young man in the torn black suit glances around our narrow arena, wall to one side, empty air on the other. The young man stares once more at us, at the bus that hit him, the bus that hit her. He raises himself on one good arm, pushes with his good arm, and like a crow he drops over into space to follow his girl-friend.

And at that moment I begin to understand the language of race and age and grief, that you can have everything at once and suddenly nothing at once, like an orange bullet train screaming past your platform in Dublin, blurred windows there in a streak you can touch and then just air ringing above the tracks, the train vanished, but that echo of reverb still hanging.

Both of them fly into space and both fall into the sea, Icarus and his pretty girlfriend hanging over the sea's glare and boats with white scar wakes and lean sails and the sea's ancient beaches pinned at the base of these stunning cliffs.

The beautiful couple falls into new worlds and now our giant plane rises toward another world, now I fly to the far west, we have liftoff, hundreds of rows of passengers thrust west in the night, air clubbing through the gnashing turbines and giant black wheels spinning as they tuck themselves up into the Boeing undercarriage, tires and turbines and rows of seated travellers strapped into a dome of stars and jet contrails and blinking lights that betray our route in the sky to those citizens who might watch below.

Our plane's route takes us high under a ghostly cupola, our plane moves inside the jet-blue ceiling of a vast starry chapel, but are we amazed?

Instead of being amazed, most of us choose to close our eyes, to drift into a preliminary form of vibrating sleep.

While held like a brain inside our plane's strange roiling motion I remember Pico toiling endlessly to serve us in the family hotel and I remember those workers digging out a cellar by hand and bucket and families unloading crates of fruit and peppers and loaves in the tin-roof market at dawn and O my love, will you and this Decembrists song always make me sad?

I remember the young woman washing the aqua tiles of my room with her hair (how I wanted her in my bed, the giant white bed floating in my tiny room, but I knew it would never happen) and in Rome they allow no high-rises and my floor tiles mimic peacock colours of the sea, mirror the collapsing wave's complex codes and sine curve and the sea's secret inhabitants.

Luke the Apostle asks us, *Who is better, the one who sits or the one who serves?* Every day we take what they offer to us, the cabin crew, the maid, the baker, the waiter, every day we take what they give us, what they serve, muttering *grazie, grazie,* as they bend to our needs, our care, our eternal care.

High above that charmed parish of villas lit by milky Italian moonlight, high above our planet, we simply sit. We do not swoon or high five. We sit and we hold serviettes to our thin lips listening to George Jones (*put your sweet lips*) or Radiohead and at our plane's tiny windows our tiny eyes swivel in the crowded heavens above that turbulent benevolent boot of an peninsula (*a little closer to the clyster pipes*), above Mediterranean waters and above Spain and we devour our last spicy repast and we turn our heads to those serving and we wonder and hope, if we ask meek as orphans might there be a little more.

And then we travel back to sleep and we travel back to the New World with ancient dreams of Rome's glory and our lack of glory and Janus giving you the eye in Trastevere and the black shamrock sprayed on a wall by my hotel and under the Vatican that naked woman showering on a rooftop and the Pope blessing her sunlit form.

Rome so beautiful, Italy so beautiful, the lunatic world so beautiful; we must embrace it purely, wantonly, for we are alive, we are free. Here is the plain truth: we are not dead at the bottom of a cliff, we are not suffocated by the volcano, no showers of stones and hot cinders fall on our heads, no knife is driven in our leg.

So why are we so sleepy? In the name of heaven, why do we not swoon, why do we orphans not high five over and over, why do we not dance and laugh every moment of each living day and night? I can't dance, but you know, just a suggestion.

Palace of the Brine
Kerry-Lee Powell

Today's the day Mitchell Burnhope gets the royal shit kicked out of him. That's the consensus at the bar. Marie-Odile's bear-shaped brothers are already brooding in the rear, chowing down on a late breakfast of hot dogs and slush puppies. Every few minutes one of them looks up at the door with his monobrow beetled.

So it's ironic, as far as Mitchell Burnhope is concerned, that today's feature dancer is Destiny. She keeps cockatiels in her room and lets them fly around uncaged. It's not unusual, a lot of dancers travel with pets. The cockatiels shit on the bedspread and on her clothes, but Destiny doesn't care or hasn't noticed. Judging from the amount of bills rolled into coke straws on her hotel-room floor and the dregs on her dressing table, she's not often in the frame of mind for righteous housekeeping. Vlada says she's a bad woman. And Vlada should know. She's made a character study of every dancer the Coronet Hotel has ever hired.

"We're all bad," I say to her. "We're strippers."

Vlada's an odd bird too. With her whiskers and hooked nose, she looks just like the kind of witch that speaks in omens and has uncanny insights. Over time I've come to realize that most of her pronouncements stem from an obsession with personal hygiene. I guess you pick up strange ideas about humanity when you've spent five years in one of Stalin's gulags.

Marie-Odile pushes past us in a butterfly kimono, wafts a trail of bubble-gum vapours in her wake. Vlada clutches my hand and mutters. I don't know what particular offence to the gods of cleanliness Marie-Odile has committed in the past, but she's made an enemy of Vlada. Marie-Odile is also my replacement.

It's unspoken, but everyone knows. Frank's been warning me for months. I haven't been on stage in six months. I'm the broad with the cleavage they keep around to mother the old boys at the back, soothe them into blowing their pay cheques on over-priced booze. One more pound on that ass, says Frank, and you're three deep in the heap.

At any rate, it's not pity that has Vlada clucking over me. Before I started stripping in the hotel club I stripped sheets, scrubbed toilets, and helped her heave around a dicky-wheeled housekeeping cart stuffed with towels and miniature soaps. For this I have earned her undying loyalty. I should get a tin star and a sickle for my hard time.

Sometimes I try to picture what this place was like before it was hacked up into smaller rooms. There are traces of old-world grandeur: peeling cherubs and the remains of a mosaic dance floor in the storeroom where I sneak cigarettes and pick at the tiles with the tips of my stilettoes. The place is sinking like Venice. Like Atlantis. Any day the city will paste a condemned sign on the entrance and the rats will pour out into the daylight. But right now we're holding out for Mitchell Burnhope to turn up in his oversized coat and get himself pounded into Beefaroni in the parking-lot.

Marie-Odile returns to her chair, the butterfly kimono fluttering behind her. She leans back and lets out a belch that resounds through the empty bar. Her brother Raoul, fake-slaps her, catching his heavily ringed fingers in her curls. Raoul and his meatier brother Hugo walked out of a Grimm's fairy tale and laid their woodsman axes at the door a couple of years back. It didn't take them long to get accustomed to their new life. Everyone in the club is terrified of them. Raoul disentangles himself with a grunt, walks over to the cigarette machine, and stabs at his cell-phone with his stubby fingers. He's trying to score a spot for Marie-Odile in an upcoming porno flick. The competition is cutthroat. A juicy role will triple a dancer's salary overnight and land her gigs in every upscale club on the circuit. This is how it is now. Big business. A whole intricate system.

In my day there were girls who dreamed about dancing in the ballet or on Broadway. Of going out west to run away from their crazy boyfriends. Girls, lazy or heartbroken, who just wanted to make the world fuzz over in their hotel room with a dose of codeine and a quart of Southern Comfort. And very rarely, girls like me, who just want their noses in a book after work with a bowl of chips and a pack of cigarettes at their elbow.

They couldn't find a chambermaid's uniform big enough to fit me when I started working here. I wasn't big on purpose, I simply never gave a thought to anything that happened below my collarbone. But cleaning rooms is hard labour. The pounds melted off, and it wasn't too long before Frank was smacking my rear and getting me up to audition with the others on amateur night. He still brags about how he rescued me. I often ask myself what's worse—grinding in a pair of crotchless panties to a bar full of wing-eating oafs or scooping up Chihuahua shit in an overheated hotel room? Most days I could go either way.

On my first shift as a chambermaid Vlada hobbled into the lobby, led me up to a room on the second floor, and flung the door as if she was opening the imperial gates to a lost civilization. Scarves and stockings were coiled around a stuffed elephant swimming in a pool of melted pink ice cream. A tipped-over jar of nail polish had drooled down the TV screen. A sequined belt nestled in a plate of gnawed steak bones beside a banana-cream pie studded with ruby-lipsticked cigarette butts. The room's centrepiece was a pyramid of clothes with a chicken carcass picked clean and perched on top. She handed me a bucket, a few garbage bags, and a carafe of cleaning supplies. She warned me to separate the rotting stuff from the makeup and clothes. Grinning, she handed me a paper sash with the word 'sanitized' stamped on it.

"Don't forget to put Miss America on the toilet."

When Vlada came back we humped the bags down to a basement storage-room that was crammed full of other garbage bags tagged with girls' names. Dancer names like Bambi and Barbarella. Every once in a while, a girl turns up in the lobby to reclaim her abandoned things, wild-eyed and rapping her car keys or fingernails on the front desk. It's amazing how many of them disappear. I asked Vlada once if she thought a cruel fate had befallen them or if they'd just turned over a new leaf.

"Either way, they go to a better place," she said, sucking the side of her cheek.

More and more often now the girls are neat as soldiers, ordering their brushes and makeup bottles into symmetrical rows. For this they earn the unseen respect of a bandy-legged, moustachioed ex-Soviet whose chief nervous tic is to stick her tongue out as far as it will stretch.

Whitney Houston comes on the sound system, and Destiny totters on stage in six-inch platform heels. She grabs the pole to steady herself and bends over backwards with an arcing fan of platinum hair.

For my first show here I made a cassette tape of corny songs and worked out a routine in the storage-room. The songs sounded wrong when I mounted the stage. At first I thought it was nerves, but the tape was damaged. I got lost in the distortions and wobbled my way to the end while a part of me watched myself transform from Helen Blackmore, winner of the inter-high school spellathon, lover of Reese's peanut-butter cups and ex-member of the youth choir, into a naked human, knock-kneed and shivering in a draft of winter air from a door some idiot had left open. I stared out at a sea of shadowy faces. I climbed down the steps after the machine ate the rest of the tape reel, the last song snarling into a wordless tangle.

Mitchell Burnhope came here on his birthday with a bunch of other young bucks trying to look sober. Not for him, the ritual jacking off into a wad of Kleenex in the booths at the back. He was going to fall in love. You could see Cupid's arrow hovering a few inches in front of his chest as he gazed around the room. Which was when Marie-Odile stepped out of the dressing-room like a fawn into a woodland bower, pausing to fix a beaded strap on her tiny ankle. The blossom of a smile on her cherry-glossed lips was all it took to plunge the arrow so deep into his chest you could see the tip poking out through the back of his cheap blazer.

The next day he turned up early and sober. He dealt out business cards embossed with his name and the word "entrepreneur" in shiny letters. It took Hugo and Raoul the amount of time it takes to flick a switchblade to measure his worth and turn their backs, bending the cards in half before tossing them into the brimming ashtrays. Soon after the flowers arrived, a matronly bouquet of chrysanthemums that sent Marie-Odile into a sulk after she tears open the box.

Later on that day I saw the abandoned flowers arranged in Vlada's old green vase down in the laundry-room. Not much happens at the Coronet without her knowing about it. She's always somewhere: a flash of grey, a bent back disappearing around the corner, the sound of a vacuum cleaner in a distant room. I feel her presence wherever I am, the way you feel mice in a wall or pigeons fluttering in the eaves. The basement laundry-room is where she makes herself at home, losing herself in reveries too painful or too lovely to talk about, smiling like a village idiot at the embroidered daisies on an old kitchen towel while the tumble dryers churn endless loads of laundry. I sat down and asked her what she thought about the unfolding love story upstairs. She pursed her lips.

"Not good," she said.

"How long do you think he'll last?"

"Who knows," she said. She smiled and let out a little cackle. "Why not ask Destiny?"

An idea infects you, occupies your mind like a virus. A St. Vitus Dance that has you jerking and twitching, laughing and weeping, dancing around the room for no apparent reason. Makes a holy fool of you. Has you tossed in vats of boiling oil and thrown to lions. Has you oblivious to the monsters slouching in loosely formed groups in a bar full of muffled grunts and a covert exchange of glances. It wasn't enough for Mitchell Burnhope to adore Marie-Odile from a distance. He wanted to save her.

He comes back again and again, alone in the oversized coat, like a man who has found Jesus, smiling and holding out his hand long after the person in front of him refuses to shake it. He sends more flowers. He sends presents. A fuzzy heart-shaped pillow with wings. A chocolate astronaut in a box lined with tinfoil stars. A googly-eyed teddy bear on a pair of pink-plastic downhill skis that Marie-Odile plops into the restaurant's kitchen garbage canister seconds after ripping off the wrapping paper.

Vlada gave me a tea set from Zellers a few years ago. A blurry willow pattern on grey-flecked china. I was just about to hand it back and tell her I didn't drink tea when I remembered her endless white coffees sloshing alongside us in the housekeeping cart. The tea set was meant to sit on a shelf looking ceremonial. Because I don't have my own place yet I keep it in the trunk next to my spare tire. The box is frayed and warped and stained with salt and antifreeze. I try to get rid of it sometimes, but whenever I dump it on the curb I feel Vlada's eyes burning holes into my head and put it straight back in the car.

Each night the club fills up with rednecks and hicks, their hair slicked back as if for church and portly salesmen in polyester suits and half the local chapter of the Hell's Angels. The girls undulate like sea anemones under the blue lights and the room is awash in booze and hormones and the stink of genitals and sweat. A slight change and the equilibrium is lost. Algae blooms. Blood spills in the emergency exits and out into the parking-lot to mingle with the asphalt and tiny pieces of grit and other people's teeth.

Have you ever had a fish tank? You've got to keep the balance right. My father had one when I was growing up. He bought it for relaxation but like everything else to do with him, it turned into a horror show. He had Japanese fighting fish maiming each other and inbred cannibal guppies and a crab that ate every other creature and then died of loneliness. He left it like that for a while, a tank full of cloudy yellow water that he stared into sometimes looking for signs of life. One night when he was drunk he smashed it with a hammer. I heard the glass crack from my bedroom, and then the sad whoosh of water. We never got the sour smell out of the carpet.

I almost couldn't look when Mitchell Burnhope came into the lobby the last time, a small velvet box in his fist, his neck sinking into his collar as he made his way to the bar where an imperious Marie-Odile sat flanked by her burly brothers.

In the room of a ransacked palace, fires guttering in the streets below, someone has an idea and tells it to an undersecretary, who jots it down and types it into a directive. Someone has an idea and then the idea has you, led at gunpoint to a train station, forced on board a cattle car, and set trundling across the tundra on a bed of dirty straw. Vlada almost never speaks of those years but when she does there's no overarching story, there's no moral or ending. A battle for a dropped crust. A night search that has her standing like a statue for hours, naked between the winter stars and the piles of frozen excrement at her feet.

I went to her apartment once. There was a bus strike and a snow-storm and, after she mentioned that she was walking in to work, I offered her a lift. All day and all the night before squalls had blasted waist-high drifts along the streets, and we drove through the white half-buried city to its farthest outreaches. I pulled up at her apartment block just as the streetlights were casting their first sallow haloes onto the still unplowed sidewalks. How she had made her way into work that morning was anyone's guess. I stared at her in stunned respect. Childless, husbandless, she was tough enough at 70 to cross the Khyber Pass.

I had a boyfriend once who worked in the merchant navy. I used to take him up to the rooms on the third floor where nobody goes now except Vlada with her rags and feather dusters. He lay on the bed, a slab of raw pink beef staring up at the ceiling. The harbours in Asia are full of girls, he said. There are so many to begin with, they start them so young and there's so much sick-ness. Most of them are washed up by the time they hit their twenties. What to do, have them crawling the alleys like diseased cats? A slit at the throat, a shove off the pier. It's almost a kind-ness.

I see it when I close my eyes, the seafloor littered with pelvic bones that settle into the sediments like spent oyster shells. Once you know something like that, how can you go on fooling your-self about anything?

The girls playing Hearts at a nearby table put their cards down to get a better look when Mitchell Burnhope went down on bended knee. He couldn't have picked a better moment. Having somehow displeased her brothers, Marie-Odile was already in a terrible temper. His grovelling shape was probably a reminder that she would also be on her knees in a few hours, bracing herself for blows after the brothers had swilled their quota of beer.

Of course she would have said no. But if he'd picked a different day, maybe she wouldn't have flown up out of her seat and kicked him so hard in the balls that he curled into a foetus around her candy-red stilettoed foot. Her curses and the mirthless chuckles of the two Goliaths on either side of her would have been enough to snuff the intentions of most suitors. Not Mitchell Burnhope. As soon as he could draw a full breath, he brushed himself off and said he wouldn't stop. Whether that meant loving her or hanging on to his death wish wasn't clear.

Destiny whirls around the pole, smiles and gestures at the mostly empty room with her free hand. Marie-Odile shivers and reties the sash of her kimono, then pats the wrinkled butterflies in her lap. Raoul and Hugo grunt and glare at the door, suck the last of their slush puppies through their straws.

After Destiny leaves the stage I slip down to the basement to chew the fat and fold towels with Vlada. Frank comes down to pester me into giving him a backrub. With his red-rimmed eyes and drooping paunch, he's easy to feel sorry for. Even if he does make a living off my naked body. Even if he is just about to fire me. He sits down at the table and watches me fold towels while Vlada clucks over him and doles out the same flavour cup-of-soup she's just prepared for me. To Vlada we're all slaves, indentured to a menacing, intricate system she's always abstractly aware of even if we're not.

She hobbles out into the corridor with a pile of folded towels. I'll take her place in a few years when her arthritis is so bad she can no longer hold a mop. Will I be strong enough to survive as long as she has?

There's a harsh cry and I run to the door.

Vlada is sprinting down the corridor as fast as her bandy little legs will carry her, shaking her fist at the tiny blur of white and yellow that flits and whizzes ahead of her. The escaped cockatiel darts around the corner.

By the time I reach them the cockatiel is in the boiler-room, flying from pipe to pipe, perching in the warm recesses of the ancient grease-encrusted furnace that not even Vlada attempts to dust. She stands there with her hands outstretched, chanting

57

a Russian nursery rhyme under her breath. The bird eyes her suspiciously.

Losing patience, Vlada pokes at it with a broom handle. The cobwebs stick to the handle and droop into ragged fringes. The cockatiel flies over to the rectangular window set into the rough concrete wall and flutters there for a moment before flying back to the pipe. Vlada coos, hands cupped and outstretched again, as if she were offering a gift. The bird is in a panic, flying back and forth, tapping its beak on the glass and then returning to clench the pipe, its tiny chest heaving.

"Fine you stupid bird," says Vlada. The cockatiel cocks its head at her. She pushes her footstool beneath the window and climbs up. Even so, she can barely reach the sash. She heaves it open with a grunt. A cascade of paint flakes, dust, and snow settle on her shoulders and the furnace-room floor. She bunches her face into a knuckle and steps down. A blast of wind sweeps in another small flurry.

"So go," she says. "Go into the dirty fucking snow and die."

It's a scene from a fairy tale: the cockatiel perched on a cob-webbed pipe with its scarlet China-doll cheeks looking down at bandy-legged Vlada with her broomstick and then back again at the window, alive with whirling snow and the sound of approaching sirens. There is a moment when even the cockatiel seems to understand what has been happening, what is always happening, beyond the borders of its birdy world. And now all eyes are on the grey-white rectangle as it blushes to pink and then cherry red, and the ambulance swings into the parking-lot.

Marriage
Rebecca Rosenblum

Just before April exams, one of my Canadian Poetry students disappeared—not just from my class but from the earth. Catherine Reindeer's purse was found in a restaurant parking-lot down by the lakefront, and she never came home. She was a good student, good enough that she didn't need me to review her essay topics or suggest background readings, so I didn't know her much. She was—is?—a pretty girl, confident, a bit older than the rest. She had a husband, the newspapers said, unusual for an undergrad. I didn't remember a ring. I hadn't really paid much attention to her, no more than to any other pretty girl. Not much more. After she was gone I thought of her constantly.

When the semester ended, I had to give Catherine an *Incomplete* and move on to teaching a summer class, which were always full of the kind of kids who were looking for an easy pass, stoners, guys who left their skateboards in the aisle. There wasn't much else going on that summer: I'd sent off my latest monograph for consideration, I was arguing with my TA, and everyone I could tolerate socially seemed to have gone to a cottage. All I had left was hosing birdshit off the patio chairs and attending the wedding of my wife's cousin.

The day of Lisha's wedding, the summer students' essays were so blithely terrible, so full of strange misreadings and so obviously concentrated on poems in the first half of the anthology, so freighted with *thuses* and *obviouslies* and misspellings of the poets' names, that it was afternoon before I even considered my clothes. It was a relief to close the study door and go across the hall to the bedroom, but the relief didn't last long. The summer suit was right at the back of my closet, where I'd left it in 2006, after the last formal wedding of a distant cousin. Somehow, since then, the jacket had gotten tight under the arms. The only comfortable way to position my hands was as if I were offering a tray of drinks. Perhaps it had always been that way and I'd forgotten; I doubted very much that my shoulders had broadened.

The bride, Lisha, was a third cousin of Gretta's whom I'd only met a handful of times, affianced to a man whose name, as far as I could recall, I was never told. I doubted they'd care much how I dressed. Anyway, several students' use of the word *confusing* to describe their own arguments had panfried my brain, and I could think of no alternative outfit, so I set off uncomfortably for the church.

Outside for the first time all day, I realized that the weather had turned; the sky had eaten the sun and our building no longer cast a shadow. Inside the car was like being inside a lung; the air was damp and thick. About three blocks out, I realized that I knew the way only hazily, and the Google Maps printout was crumpled on my office floor. I turned onto 3rd Concession anyway, full speed down to the lake, directions be damned— Gretta would know. She grew up in that pale grey suburb where people on the radio were always commenting that schools were underfunded.

Traffic was as sticky and dense as the air. Even with the air-conditioning on and the windows sealed, I could still feel the humidity creeping in. There were university kids all over, wandering off the sidewalks, weaving slowly between cars stopped at lights, pausing in the middle of crosswalks to yell to each other and squint into the sky. Summer session was almost over, but down by the water with the shops selling used CDs and hemp bars and complicated swimsuits, school was never much of any issue, anyway.

I passed the restaurant where Catherine had been last seen, the one she worked at. It gave no sign of its dramatic role. The chalkboard out front advertised specials of fajitas and 2-for-1 martinis. The patio was crowded. As I passed in the crawling traffic, a big guy with a soft blond beard was standing to pour from a pitcher.

Even though it was only 3:01, Gretta was already at the curb in front of her shop, looking south with her body arched forward.

She'd changed her clothes since the morning, from jeans to a long purple silk dress, fading in and out of wallpaper shades, from pale to brilliant, violet to lilac. It was shapeless and sleeveless and hung away from her body as she tilted on the sidewalk. Her much younger assistant had given her the high-heeled sandals. They were tied with ribbons crisscrossing her shins, up and under her hemline. The whole outfit, the dull dangling earrings, her hair loose down her back—it all made her seem younger than she was, and different, too. I knew she would be uncomfortable in an hour, sooner, as soon as anyone looked at her. I knew that soon she'd be sorry she'd worn any of it.

All this before the car had even come to a complete stop. She entered with a heavy whiff of grape gum, slammed the door, put on her seatbelt. Her bag slid to the floor with a fabric-muffled *thunk* that could have been either books or wood.

I put the car into gear and started moving. "Hi, Gretta."

"Len."

"I'm fine, thanks."

"Didn't we say two-thirty?"

I bit the inside of my cheek. "Three."

"Yes, and then we remembered cottage traffic and so...."

"Two-thirty?"

"Yes."

"At least this wasn't one of the times I decided on your behalf that you wouldn't mind waiting. I just forgot."

She flicked on the radio, twisted the dial, flicked it off. "The 414 onramp is up ahead. It's a left merge." A beat. "You should get over."

"Yeah, I know."

She shifted, hunching toward the window.

It wasn't until we were finally on the 414 and through the trauma of the merge that I realized I hadn't actually apologized for my lateness. That ship had sailed, so I tried, "You have a good day?"

Gretta rolled down her window and spat her gum into the weeds and gravel beside the road as we whooshed by.

"I thought the beadwork was just lovely." That was Denise talking, some cousin of both Gretta and the bride, very feathered hair and fluty voice. Everyone was conversing along those lines, though. "She still had that soft, flowy look, the dress didn't get weighted down with beads." There seemed to be a lot to say about that particular wedding dress. Lisha truly did have that ascending-angel look all young blond brides have, but that was her, not the dress. Maybe it was just a boring reception, or a reception of boring people with nothing else to talk about but lace and seed pearls and taffeta. I hadn't contributed anything to the conversation but smiling, currently with closed lips over the too-big bite of hot crabcake.

Other than that, I had been drinking champagne in alternation with scotch and soda, and waiting for some interesting ironies to emerge from attending a wedding with my wife without speaking to her. The whole conceit had been a letdown so far. Gretta didn't let me indulge in any sort of arm-linking, hand-holding, or other for-appearances minor affections that might have made the evening seem elegantly sad. She watched me with the same tolerance she did at home, left six inches between us in the pew, and looked exhausted when people hugged her thin shoulders. I found myself feeling almost homesick for Gretta, though I knew she was somewhere in that same big room, likely eating a crabcake of her own.

"I think they'll be happy, don't you? Now that Kieran's got such a good job and everything." Denise's hair was cut or pinned into wings in front of her ears, as if her head might fly. Behind her, through enormous panes of glass, the night lawn of the golf course was navy and silver and tempting.

"Oh, yes, good job—ticket to a happy marriage." I set down my drink to slice a large wedge of Brie from the round on the buffet.

Denise looked at me with bright attention, as if I'd just entered the room. "I only meant...I mean, it helps."

"Of course, yes." I put a fistful of crackers into a napkin with the cheese, in preparation for fleeing out the patio doors.

"Where's Gretta?"

"Gretta?" One of the crackers slipped from its napkin, bounced on the floor and hopped under the hem of Denise's long skirt. She pretended not to notice.

"Your wife?" Denise grinned and punched me—gently, but

not that gently—in the shoulder. More crackers went skittering.

"Oh—sorry, Denise, could you just—" She obediently took the napkin full of crumbs. I scanned the room, brushing off my hands. "Gretta, she's—" I saw the bleached tablecloths, the polished dark wood floor, a couple who had been at my own wedding, a young woman with dark gleaming hair just like Catherine's.

At last: "There." I pointed toward a window glinting pink with the setting sun, almost directly across the hall from us. Gretta was standing neatly against the high windowsill, ankles tight together in her dreamy shoes. She was talking to a tiny brunette, who was bouncing a tiny brown-haired baby in her arms.

"Oh. What a striking dress! So many different purples."

I bristled slightly—I would have used the same tone to describe that dress, but a husband has certain privileges. "Is that Mary? When did she have another baby?"

"Where have you been?"

I flapped a hand. "Oh, you know, the urban jungle." Mary was just tipping her arms against Gretta's to pass the flailing child over. Gretta was biting her lip, shifting her sharp elbows; uncomfortable, uncuddly Gretta.

"They're calling her Emily."

Gretta's bare arms in the last blaze of sun were a similar colour to the pale pink bundle she was holding. Her dress clashed with the blanket and was already rumpled. She passed the baby back to Mary as quickly as she could, but gently. She had only glanced at the tennis-ball head. Mary strolled off to more willing admirers. Denise moved down the buffet, smiling at someone in the distance.

Gretta was staring into space, space that after a moment included me. She frowned. I tipped my head in Mary's direction and smiled. She shrugged, then turned to take a glass of champagne from a waiter with a tray of them. He said something and Gretta nodded, laughed, said something too. He grinned, then moved off into the crowd, offering his wares.

That could have been me.

I remember what it was like to be young—a child, even. I remember the best seat on the bus is the one above the wheel well, for the footrest, for the rarity. I remember the tilt of my hand on a sweatered waist at a dance, I remember the answering smile that meant *go, stay, I like you, dance with me, go, go*. I remember the crunch of gravel and blotches of ink on exam papers and bright blue superheroes falling from the sky. I remember how it is to lead a life worth remembering.

I've seen photos of Gretta from the yearbook years. Seen her standing, prom-dress proud in an over-decorated living-room, or lying laughing in pile of bronze leaves. And the other stranger shots, where her eyes are canted down, or she's drawn a book or her hair over her face. She was sometimes shyly veiled and other times simple and sure, so no-one knew what to make of her. So she made it of herself.

I've also seen her, head bent and hair twisted tightly at her nape, reading on the chesterfield—she still calls it that. The book is in her lap and she dangles her upper body over it, her bare narrow feet propped on the ottoman. Her worn terry robe slips apart at the hem, letting the lamplight gleam off her dry, shaved shins. I try to tell myself that the girl with cakes and bouquets and diplomas was always walking toward me, always on her way to becoming what she is now, mine, but the imagination won't reach that far. I could have loved her then, perfectly, unreservedly, and we never even knew it.

It was raining when we finally left the reception. We had stayed longer than either of us had wanted, I'm sure, owing to pathetic inability to find each other in the big dark hall. By the time we reunited, diffidently, too tired not to be comforted by a familiar face, the rain had turned the gravel parking-lot into a grey soup. I was a step ahead of Gretta going down the stairs and as I sloshed through, my mind was on the ruin of my only good teaching loafers. I was halfway across before I realized Gretta hadn't followed me outside; someone had stopped her way back at the doorway.

I was already so wet that more rain didn't matter, although on another day I would likely have cared anyway. Sitting in the rain suited my mood, so I went the rest of the way to the car, sat down on the hood to watch her finally walk down the cement stairs to the parking-lot. The someone from the doorway escorted her down with his hand on the inside of her elbow.

She looked around in the shadows, for me, presumably. He— whoever he was—drew his hand off her arm to shield her face from the rain. It seemed to me that his fingers brushed her hair, that he smiled in a way that assumed that because she couldn't find me, I wasn't there. And she smiled back, and then I made my fingers into a megaphone and shouted, "Gretta!"

Her eyes were on me for a few seconds before she saw me. He turned and said something while already walking away. Gretta shrugged and started to dash across the parking-lot through the slicing rain. Her dress clung like...well, there's nothing better than wet silk. Of course it was too dark to make out any details of panties, nipples, thighs, but I knew them well enough that I didn't have to.

Likewise, I didn't see her ankle turn in the rutted gravel, but it was easy to imagine when I saw her tumble, almost as if she were falling off her high shoe. Of course, she couldn't fall off it; it was tied to her, so her ankle wrenched and she fell hard onto her stomach and elbows, feet splayed. Then she lay as still as a stage prop.

Just for a moment I thought about the ruin of her purple silk dress. In the dark and the rain, it looked as grey as anything else, and with the mud, soon it would be. But it had been pretty— inappropriate, but pretty. Most other women in their forties would've looked far worse in it. I startled to recall, as she lay there, that I was a man with a beautiful wife; somehow it had always been something hard for me to remember. I slid off the hood and splashed over.

"Okay?" I tugged her to her feet, her wire-tight fingers digging into mine.

"Yeah." The rain on her face was too profuse and speckled with dirt to mistake for tears, yet it did remind me of them. "Yeah, I'm fine." But she limped back to the car, favouring the twisted ankle.

She sat in the passenger seat without comment, gaze on the ceiling. I put the car into gear and flicked on the lights, thinking about the upholstery. And tolerance. And marriage. And that guy, whoever he was, in the parking-lot. The silence greenhoused in the sealed damp car.

I couldn't judge the space between oncoming cars, so I waited for complete darkness—no headlights—before pulling into the road. Out of the corner of my eye, I saw Gretta run her fingers down her seatbelt and touch the buckle.

I dug my fingertips into the hard plastic steering wheel, watched the hyphenated centre line flutter past, and finally muttered, "Long night," before I turned on the radio.

It was the crackle of news, not what I wanted in the humid car. But Gretta cocked her head away from the window toward the words *plea* and *police*, and went so far as to touch my hand to still it when I went for the dial. Her fingers were winter-cold and her wet hair slid swampily down her shoulder and I let her listen.

There was nothing new—Catherine was the same degree of missing as on the 5 o'clock report. The night was gleaming with rain and it was soothing to watch things flipping by the windows too blurred to think about.

"Still missing. It's been three weeks," she said.

"Hmm?"

"That girl. This girl they're talking about. Catherine Reindeer. The missing one."

Police encourage anyone having potential information on her whereabouts to come forward. I wondered to myself what "potential information" might be, but all I said was, "No, more—a month." 34 days.

Even though Catherine was always on the news, and no-one in town didn't know about her disappearance, abduction, whatever we were calling it (not murder), it seemed strange to hear Gretta say her name, like she had drawn something out of my subconscious and said it aloud.

What else could she see, inside my brain? Catherine in a burgundy tank top with the right strap pushed off her shoulder, onto her biceps. Catherine stretching, arms toward the ceiling and the thick padded strap of her backpack pushing her shoulder strap low. Did I even truly remember this, or was it my mind grasping. "I'd...I'd give her an extension."

"What?"

I stopped for an amber light, and in the streetlight glow I could see the demise of that inconvenient dress: drenched and twisted, torn to reveal a slice of muddy knee.

"On her final paper. She missed it, and the exam too, but...."

"Oh, Len." She tipped her forehead against the streaked window. "She was your student. How did I not know this?"

It was strange how stricken she was, as if she suddenly knew just how hard I'd been thinking about Catherine's absence all this time. Her cold fingertips tapped my wrist again, even softer this time, as if she knew everything.

I couldn't return the favour and read Gretta's mind—I didn't know what she was thinking with her eyes closed against the cold window. Probably she assumed the missing girl and I had been close, that I was privately devastated by the loss. And since the devastation was true, it seemed irrelevant that Catherine Reindeer had come to my office only to pick up a few marked assignments, raised her hand in class a few times to give some forgettable answers about prosody, rebellion, Leonard Cohen. But I remembered her, a girl in a burgundy tank top over brown skin. I remembered her standing up in the second row of the lecture hall watching me gather my notes, shuffle them, drop them. She stood with her hands stretched above her head, the burgundy strap sliding while a kid in a ballcap asked me about library reserves. She put the thick padded straps of her backpack over her shoulders and they matched the straps of her shirt for a few inches, then tucked under just where her breasts started to curve out. And the tension of that class where none of the kids seemed to be doing well, and me not knowing when the reserve desk closed, and the slope of her stomach.

The possibility that she was dead had blasted all that hazy memory with a backwards light. The thick swimming rain on the road, headlights glinting off what should have been just air but was water. Her breasts curving out from the twisted strap, hand smoothing it down as she turned to face me. A eulogy I could never give—didn't even know her major. Her thick-fingered hand waving to me as she turned to leave. No-one thought I knew her because I didn't, really. Only watched, and remembered.

It was raining so heavily that the windshield looked like it was sliding away. Gretta's hand on my shoulder. Catherine wasn't dead. As long as no-one knew for sure, then she wasn't. No-one knew anything. "Len!" Flash of headlights. Brown skin, only lost—the bush and forest outside of town was vast. "Len!"

I swerved from the blond headlights bearing down on us, way too late, just in time. A spray of wet gravel sluiced up as I blurred onto the shoulder. I wasn't thinking, thank God, just watching the dull face of the safety wall pull closer, braking, swerving, clutching the wheel, Gretta's steadying hand on my shoulder. It only took five, maybe ten seconds to be driving on the asphalt again. I carefully ducked my shoulder out from under her hand, so she wouldn't feel me shaking. It was another ten minutes home. All silent.

I parked under a street-lamp, sloppily, still shaking. Gretta leaned limply against the rain-dark window, but turned toward me when I turned toward her.

"Am I drunk? I didn't think I was drunk, but I just didn't— Am I?"

Gretta touched my cheek with fingers that were somehow, after a half hour in the warm dry car, still icy-wet. "My darling, I don't know."

Stragglers
Adrian Michael Kelly

My molar, it hammered me. I groped for the clock, and turned the yellow-green glow of its hands away. 3:15 AM. Go and get some Orajel, or put an aspirin on it, but we had no hallways, only rooms. Dad would hear.

I waited.

––––––––

We lived behind the Acropolis. Our landlords were the owners, and I could hear them in there now. Elena sang a song in Greek, stacking plates and saucers. Nik fried an onion. He always did that first. The smell of it bustled sharp and strong through the heating vent. I got out of bed. Any normal Saturday, we were already up an hour, and slogging down the road.

––––––––

Dad was having apnea. I peed loud and flushed, and had a look at my tooth in the mirror. The gum beneath it bulged. I pressed it and I tasted it, the poison of myself. A pair of aspirin in my palm. One I swallowed at the fridge with skim. The other I wedged right in the hole. My mouth knew to make more spit.

––––––––

Onion filled the flat now. I opened the door and screen. Rain pocked the river. In for a landing on the embankment came a fat and filthy gull. It waddled underneath the deck, where torn-open bags of Acropolis trash filled the big blue stinking bins. Other gulls were scrumming there. That hideous heads-up gape-beak screaming.

———

Dad yawned and did a fart. I went to his door.
Tea?
Aye.
Cream of Wheat?
Eggs how bout?
Hard or soft?
Soft, mine.
Soldiers too?
He did the English. I say, soldiers *do* sound jolly good.
I said, Indubitably, but when I filled the kettle up, my hand shook, my whole arm.

———

More tea? I said.
Time we got that car unloaded.
Raining pretty hard.
Made of sugar?
No.
Right. Let's get it done.
Dad was an odd combination, part-time on the ambulance, full-time painter-decorator. The Bel Air smelt of Varsol. Ladders rode the roof. We took them off, and chained them to the railing around the deck. Rain dripped from our noses. Dropsheets big as sails and heavy, gallons and quarts and pints of paint, the machine for stippled ceilings, we unloaded all of that, and plunked it on the kitchen floor. I pulled the cling of my T-shirt free.
Shower now? I said.
Aye. Don't dilly-dally.
I stepped around the tools and gear in soaking wet sock feet. Imagine if I fell. All these hard and edged things.

———

Pink and clean as new pork cutlets. I put on my Wrangler jeans. The brown plaid Western dress shirt. Tomorrow I hadn't decided. The one was a real Bill Rodgers singlet. It had a blue band across the chest. The famous BR logo. Dad got it me in Boston. The other was from my school. A gift from VP Evans. Heck of a thing you're doing, son. Hope you'll be our ambassador. The shirt was yellow as corn on the cob. Halfway down the front it had a tall green pointy star. Skinny letters in the star said p H s. No-one would have a clue what they meant, but I had red shorts with a yellowy stripe, and none with any blue. The longest time I stood there, staring at one and then at the other. Finally went with yellow and green. Ambassador of what.

———

Dead leaves plastered Highway 30. We passed the Klaussen farm. Holstein cows, their udders and their arses caked, plodded up a slant of mucky barnyard. High in the air over Pine Ridge, a hawk tilted in the wind and rain. Dad rolled down his window. The wiper had started to stagger. He reached out, and gave it a flick. Then he sniffed.

Fuck no.

I looked at the gauge. The lean of the needle.

He banged the dash. Filthy *cunt*.

I sank in my jacket.

———

We pulled in at the Shell near Brighton. Dad got out and popped the hood. Squalls of steam escaped. Round to the back of the wagon he went, and swung the tailgate open. Cool air rushed inside the car. He unlatched his First Aid kit. Took out tape and gauze and swabs, a pad.

You, he said. Off your arse.

I met him round the front.

He said, Get your coat off. Hold it up and keep this dry.

The radiator hose had split. He swabbed it like a dirty wound. Applied the sterile pad. Wrapped gauze around it. Then the tape. My arms ached. The back of me, soaked. He lowered the hood.

Wait in the car.

Came back with a brimming bucket. Uncapped the rad, and filled it.

To have talons and wings and far-seeing eyes. To think just perfect hawk thoughts.

———

In the slow lane on the 401, he kept it under 60. Truckers passed and shot us looks. The car was trailing scarves of steam. Up the way on the other side, I saw the yellow Fifth Wheel sign, and I pointed to it. Dad whacked the blinker. At the exit, turned left on a red. Ahead of us, a transport crept, belching black exhaust. Dad pulled out and had a look. Passed on a solid line. We rolled to the edge of the Fifth Wheel lot, and the car let go its last. I stared at wet macadam.

Needin a pee?

I shook my head.

Wait here, then. Won't be long.

He walked through a puddle as big as our flat, and didn't seem to notice. The camera was in his Adidas bag. When he had gone inside, I pointed it at my face. I hate this, I said, and I don't want to be here, but I didn't press the trigger. I didn't have the guts. Anyway it had no mic. I would be a silent movie. You would have to read my lips.

———

We split a Kit Kat. I chewed on the side with less decay, and waited for him to talk. He only sat there, quiet as crags.

I said, What's happening?

He said, How do you mean?

We going home?

He looked at me. Kiddin?

I didn't speak.

Denny's on his way, he said.

What about the car?

It'll have to be towed.

Are we getting it back?

He stared out his side.

———

Not to tell it now was hard, but I had promised her. After the wedding, when we had a few days, mum took me to the track. Her fat bald bookie gave us tips, but I bet on my hunches. Seven hundred was my half. We opened my first bank account. The balance was earning interest. I thought he would feel it. I thought he would see. My face was scarlet. Words were storming my throat and mouth, but I quelled them. I was rich.

———

He looked at his Seiko.
Fuck's Denny?
The rain had gone for a coffee break. I said,
Out and walk?
Aye. Good idea.
We swung our arms, and stretched. Feeble sun showed its face. Gulls mobbed the Fifth Wheel bins, and fought for scraps in the parking-lot. Through diesel fumes and fryer grease came whiffs of Lake Ontario, a cold stew of seaweed and half-rotten fish. Then a horn honked. Denny flashed his lights. I waved high and hard.
Gaw son look at the size of ye.
Iain didn't come?
He's in Long Island. Your dad no tell ye?
I shook my head.
Tournament, said Denny. You'll see him Sunday night. C'mon hop in. Car's warm.
I'll just get my bag.
Leave it, son. I'll get it.
He and dad shook hands.
Pal.
How are ye?
It made me want a brother. The history in their eyes.

———

Eighty miles an hour, and the Le Sabre felt like CP Air, cruising altitude. A wall ran along the far right lane, and Denny pointed past it. Mud and model homes.

I'm puttin carpet in half these places.

Dad only nodded.

Clamorin for trades.

No doubt they are.

I know a guy, Ahmed. His son plays wi' Iain. Hell of a foot. Anyway, he's a painter. Remember Joyce McClure?

No.

Blond wee thing. Markham Road.

Peterhead?

That's her. Done all right, Joyce has. Royal E. LePage. Her youngest plays wi' Iain too. Along at a game the other day, she says to Ahmed, Come round mine for an estimate, like? He says, You couldn't afford me. She says, Beg your pardon? He says, You couldn't afford me. The face on her. Know what I mean? I says to him after, Ahmed, could you no gie her a break? He says, Denny, I get what I'm worth. Take a guess.

No idea.

Twenty-five.

An hour? I said.

Aye son. An hour.

Dad squared his shoulders. Thinkin of backin off on the paintin. Go full-time on the ambulance.

That right?

Dunno yet.

Denny looked in the rearview mirror. How 'bout you?

Me?

Aye. How do you feel?

About what Uncle Denny?

Movin back here.

I looked at Dad. At his neck, the creases.

Where we are is fine, I said.

Talking stopped til Agincourt.

———

The street made a circle round a small park, where an old man

watched his bony mutt squeeze out spindly turds. We pulled in
the drive. Aunty Ag was watching us out the picture window,
arms crossed under her big cone breasts.

Come let me see ye.

I pecked her cheek.

Skinny malinky. She looked at Dad. No feed'n this wan?

Your accent's fadin.

She made a fist. Shut that door. Ma heat's fly'n oot.

Heat on for?

Baltic the day. Shoes! Anywan marks ma carpet, I'll brain him.

Bet you've missed this, Denny winked.

Have yez had a bit tae eat?

Could do with a bowl of soup, said Dad.

Right. Denny'll take yez doon the stair.

Into the perfect house we went. Even the basement smelled
of Glade.

———

I was allowed an Irn Bru. The soup was beef and barley. Warm
rolls as well. Came a lull in the blether, and Aunty Ag said,

Do ye hear from your sister?

I looked at Dad.

He was out to Calgary a month ago.

Thanks. I was ask'n him.

Dad gave a nod.

For the wedding, I said.

Aunty Ag stopped chewing. Whose?

Jeanette.

You're jok'n.

No.

Age is she now?

Twenty-one?

God in Heaven. She looked at Dad. Why have you no telt us?

He shrugged. Forgot.

Who's the fella?

Gord, I said.

Gord what?

Meagher.

What does he do?

Plays hockey.

Professional?

Semi. In Spokane.

Where's tha?

Washington State, said Uncle Denny. Jeanette movin there?

I don't know. Guess so.

It got quiet, but Aunty Ag said it.

Was your mum at the wedd'n?

Yes, I said. My chest was tight. Jeanette's dad as well.

Together ye mean?

Agnes, said Denny.

I'm only ask'n.

No, I said. He has a new wife.

How is your mum?

Spoiled him, said Dad.

Aye, first time she's seen him in—

Agnes, said Denny. Leave it.

We ate. Current hummed in the clock on the wall.

———

In the unfinished part of the basement, I turned on the bare light
bulb, and knelt in front of the cubby-hole. Evel Knievel, G.I.
Joe, Big Jim, Batman, Stretch Armstrong, and Star Wars characters (even the cantina creatures) were jumbled together in two
milk crates. I slid them out, and scooched in for a look at the
stack of games. Simon was on top. The batteries worked. Cross-
legged on the cool grey floor, I began to play. Four coloured tabs,
red, yellow, blue, and green, each with its own sound, lit up in
random sequence. You had to repeat the sequence by pressing
on the tabs. It started slow and easy, say, red, blue, blue, green,
but the more you got right, the faster and longer the sequences
got, red-red-blue-green-blue-yellow-red, on and on, more and
more. There is a kind of trick to it. Don't stare at the tabs. Let
your eyes go soft. Let your hand remember. Only into Level 4
could the computer begin to beat me.

———

Dad thumped down the stairs. Fuck's that?

Game.

Get it off.

Sorry.

Togs, he said, and nodded at the finished room.

We're going for a run?

Bit a film is all.

I thought today was resting.

Half a wee lap a the street.

In we went and changed. Wearing my shorts and shirt felt wrong, like premature delivery. I thought they might be angry, and take revenge tomorrow, siphon off my strength. In my head I told them sorry. Asked them for permission, and promised we wouldn't be long. I wouldn't sweat, or get them dirty. Right back in the bag they'd go. Resting. Til tomorrow.

———

Denny blew on his hands. Sure ye want to do this now?

Dad shrugged. Sun's out.

Give us the camera, then.

I'll get the lad on his own first.

Fine. I'll scratch my arse.

Dad ignored him, and looked at me. Top of the street. Run back.

I cut through the park at a medium jog. Rust speckled the swing-set. A Becker's bag blew by, and caught in a wobbling bush. Then I stepped in a squish of shit. Scraped my shoe on the curb, and retched. Dad was waving, *Go*. I gave the legs a little gas, but before I entered the final bend, he had taken the camera away from his face, and I saw the disgusted slits of his eyes.

Back, and do it again.

Wrong wi' it? said Denny.

Again, said Dad. Put some umph in it.

Have ye asked him if he wants to?

The face on Dad.

Denny looked at me. Eh son? Do ye want to do this now?

I nodded.

Just say—

77

Uncle Denny. It's all right.

This time I got set, and took off like track. A 1500 metre pace. Into the bend I went even harder.

OK kid. Got it.

I pretended not to hear him.

Ease up, he said. EASE UP.

Those half-seconds. When both my feet are off the ground. When I'm full-out, and the air is streaming.

———

Downstairs in the finished room, he pointed to the floor.

Here.

I stood where he said, and saw it coming. BANG, above the ear.

What in fuck was that?

You said put some umph in it.

Could have pulled a muscle.

We don't even have a projector.

BANG, opposite side.

It's true.

BANG, back on the left. Anything else to tell me?

No.

Eh?

Sorry.

Go and give your face a wash. Comb that hair as well.

Off he went upstairs. In the basement washroom, I ran the taps a while, and put an aspirin in my molar. It was a lie what he told Uncle Denny. Full-time needed EMCA. He had passed the practical, but completely bombed the written. Could barely even spell.

———

Big spaghetti nosh-up. My belly out to here. I helped Aunty Ag with the dishes, then she and Denny went to get dressed. They were off to a *ceilidh* come eight o'clock. *Sha-Na-Na* would be on telly now, but Dad told me to come downstairs.

Here, he said. Get this in you.

78

It looked like a square of Jersey Milk. I asked him what it was.

Laxative, he said.

I'm not bunged up.

Flushes you out. Won't have to stop tomorrow.

We just carbo-loaded.

So?

Will I not poo them out?

Don't be daft. Mild, that. Works overnight.

You taking one?

Course I am.

I did the English. *Down* the hatch.

———

In the living-room. Full regalia, Denny. The shine of him, the swish. His sporran had a face. I asked him it.

He said, Stoat, and fiddled with his Pentax. Handed it to Dad.

Wait til the flash—

I can manage.

In came Aunty Ag. A matching kilt and sash. I said,

You look smashing.

She curtsied, Thank you, son, and put her arm round Denny.

Oor first night oot in ages, pal.

Dad said, Ready? and counted three. My aunt and uncle smiled. It wasn't fake. It was married. Away they went trailing after-shave and perfume. Dad put the telly on. I had never seen *CHiPs* in colour.

———

To tread on the carpet would have been sin. It still had the Hoover marks. No damp towels, twists of ginch. No wrinkles and no dust. Posters of Styx, Kevin Keegan, and a Glasgow Celtic scarf and strip, were pinned to the walls but perfect, like geometry. On the desk, a globe. *Encyclopaedia Britannica.* Not once had I ever been in this room, even when Iain was here. *Wish Book* room. Perfect room. I turned off the light. On the ceiling, planets and stars glowed green-yellow. I closed the door, and went downstairs, where Dad was gargling Listermint. He didn't brush at all anymore. It only made him bleed.

———

Falling asleep, he twitched and flailed, swore in slashing whispers. I lay rigid on my back, thinking he would wallop me, maybe even strangle me. At last came his snore. I nodded off, but woke with a clench and ache in my guts. Slow as a hostage, I eased out the bed, and on the way to the toilet, let slip a fart. The shock of it. The burst. I bolted the rest of the way, and barely got sat down. Soft shit blasted out of me. Then a spray of muddy flecks. Dollops of Grey Poupon in my ginch. I stared at them aghast. Didn't flush. Stuck my head out, and listened. He hadn't wakened. A bag lined the wastebin. Maybe ten minutes I took on the stairs. Every creak an agony. Gently out the side door. Feet cold against flagstone. Wind on my bare and burbling arse. I threw the bag like plastic parachute army men. It landed plop on the roof next door.

———

I made a bed of the bathroom mats. Aunty Ag had great towels, very soft and thick. One I folded and made my pillow. The other was my blanket. Every ten minutes for the first while, I was up and on the crapper, farting out my dregs. Then it got better. I thought stoats should be stoats, not sporrans, and finally, I slept.

———

My body was its own alarm. I heard him yawn and stretch.
Son?
Shot up, and turned on the light. Flushed away the thick shit pudding.
Can I get in?
Minute please.
I sorted the mats and one of the towels and wrapped the other around my waist. Gave my face a splash.
Come on, boy. I'm bustin.

Gaped my eyes as wide as I could, and pasted on a grin.

Morning!

Shh. Not so loud.

Sorry.

I ducked by. In he went for his number two. I put on my shorts, and lay on the floor, one leg extended, the other pulled toward my chest. Dad shaved. To clean his razor of bristles and cream, he slooshed it in the steaming sink, then tapped it on the edge. Usually three. Tap-tap-tap. Today it wasn't like that. Today it was idiot morse. Denny lent him styptic.

———

We lined up well back in the field, and pinned our numbers on. Dad was 1454. I was 1456. A short man right in front of me had curly hair like McEnroe, and the back of his light blue T-shirt said, *Warning: I spit left*. The Labatt logo was everywhere. A cop on a horse, its rippling rump. Denny had taken our photograph beside the statue of Edward VII, but I forgot until I saw it later. The stink of portable toilets. I remember that. Anything solid I would have sicked up, but breakfast had been electrolytes, dissolved in a glass of water.

Calm now, lad. Big deep breaths.

Vicious wind, I said.

Find someone. Tuck in behind.

Up ahead, the gun went off. A lot of the other runners cheered. We inched along. Then a slow jog.

Remember what I've telt you. Nine minute miles.

Nine minute miles.

Fluids.

Every station

Two cups at least.

Two cups at least.

Here now was the START.

This is us, he said.

This is us, I said.

Look for me out the Leslie Spit.

I will.

He pulled away.

I put one foot in front of the other, but it was bad as dreams. Hardly any grab. In the shadow of these buildings. Then I saw my uncle. He was taking film. Pumped his fist. I found my legs. Felt the crowd. Five deep and cheering. In front of Sick Kids Hospital, a gaggle of Brazilians in yellow and green saw me and went bonkers, waving their big flag. My downtown splits were eight minutes per. I couldn't help it. Total strangers, stretching over the barricades, telling me way to go, wanting me to touch their hands.

―――――

At the end of University, we veered left, past the Royal York Hotel, then down and along the lake. A different city here, all rust and blackened concrete, oil drums and cargo ships. Not so many spectators. The stink of sewage and exhaust. I remember a street called Cherry. Then a left on Unwin. Thumping wind blew cold off the lake. I squinted against the grit, and tucked in back of a tall bald guy.
   Making me do all the verk.
   We can change it up next mile.
   Stay. Vind is bitch. You are from Brazil?
   No. It's my shirt.
   They go crazy seeing you.
   Gave me a lift.
   Attention. Long vay to go.

―――――

Around the seven mile mark, we turned onto the Leslie Spit, a bare flat finger of two-lane road. Water cups rolled and skittered. A cap went wheeling past. Somebody yelled, *This is fucked!* Waves rammed the breakwater. BOOM, the spray blew in my eyes. Then the bald man barked in pain, and hobbled off the road, clutching his cramped hamstring. I leaned into wind like a hill, and remembered Calgary, where my longest run was a lazy five, every day a different mall.

―――――

Dad saw me first. He had made his turn at the end of the Spit, and now was coming back the way, shouting my name, clapping hard.

That's the way, boyo! Head up, now!

In a blink he was by, but I felt brand new, fully fuelled, and started passing people. Whapped the top of the orange stanchion when I made my turn. Now the wind was at my back. It gave me a couple of freebie miles, 7:40 per. I shouted *You can do it* to runners still coming down the way, but not so many heard. I was still alto. A single twist of pubic hair.

About mile nine I felt my nipples, tender and raw. I tugged and tented my T-shirt. Come the eleven mile mark, I was cursing it, and wishing I had worn the Bill Rodgers singlet, its soft blue band. I poured cups of water down my neck. Then in the crowd near mile twelve, I saw a boy, older than me, with a black buzz cut and headcase grin. He said, How long did you train for this? It was odd, but I answered him. Four months. He shouted after me, *You'll never make it.* The breath in me fled. I stumbled. He may as well have thrown a stone, a spear, a lightning bolt. It scrambled all my circuitry. Only the foulest Glanisburgh bams would ever had said a thing like that, the dropouts and the potheads, the juvies and the brawlers. I looked back, and there he was, still leering at me. Into my head rushed all the things I could have shouted back at him. *Fuck you. Pugface. Idiot.* I told myself *settle*—a stitch coming on—and did what dad taught me, lengthened my stride, deepened my breath. Extend your wrists, breathe in. Flex your wrists, breathe out. It's a way to remind yourself. Extend, in. Flex, out. The side-stitch faded, but a sludge of fatigue was filling my legs. I had gone out too fast, and ahead of me now was the Don Valley Parkway, miles of steady, sapping incline. I looked down my T-shirt. Both nipples bled.

There were patches of autumn to the left of me, and a gigantic black-girdered bridge. Mostly I remember road. Every mile

83

harder now than the one before. Ten yards up and to the right, a woman in purple shorts kecked. Then it came, a stringy yellow soup, swinging from her bottom lip. She tried to keep going, but wobbled. Two volunteers ran over to catch her. I heard one say, Did you see that boy? She meant my shirt, the bloodstains. I peeled it off, and kept on slogging, hoping for a second wind. Gremlins and devils and genies of pain were escaping their caves way down in my body. They gnawed and rammed. They howled. I thought to try and sing songs in my head. The only one that came to me was *Message in a Bottle*. I sang it anyway.

———

Don Mills Rd, the blue sign said. It was another turnaround point. A volunteer was gesturing like ground crew at airports. To make the hairpin round the stanchion, I had to slow right down, and very nearly stopped. Not because I thought to. My legs were giving out. My heartbeat was arrhythmic. I wondered was it possible—can someone eleven die?—but I didn't stop. I thought, Next streetlight, and made it that far.

Now, one more.

Come on. One more.

———

Ahead of me, a runner laughed.

Another one said, *Look*.

I lifted my head, and blinked.

Up on the giant black-girdered bridge, a man and woman in white were waving. The woman had wings, tin-foil wings, and a big blond cloud of curls. The man held a shepherd hook, and grinned through a bushy Godbeard. He pointed the hook straight at me, and said something to the woman.

She blew me a kiss.

I had run under and well past the bridge before I even heard the bus.

———

84

It rolled along beside me, a boxy green and white old thing. In the windows, faces. I remembered some from the Leslie Spit. Then the folding doors opened. A silver-haired man stood in the stairway.

Hello, he said.

His accent was English, and his smile an effort. The eyes on him, blue infliction.

Could you board the bus, please?

No, thank you. I'm fine.

Afraid you must. Regulations.

What regulations?

We're picking up the stragglers.

I'm not a straggler.

He tapped his watch. Oh yes you are.

No, I said.

Pardon me?

I have to finish.

Now, look here.

Someone on the bus said, Leave him alone.

The Englishman wagged his finger. You haven't seen the last of me, and waved the driver on.

I winced through a wall of diesel exhaust.

———

He picked them off one and two at a time. A few hung their heads. Others looked happy. Now the bus waited in the middle of the road.

Listen you. They have to re-open the freeway.

I pointed to the shoulder. Lots of room there.

I have strict instructions.

No.

Don't make me—

Bugger off.

Tell him, kid!

You *will* get on—

I WANT TO FINISH.

He rushed at me like a blindside flanker, but I am good at fending, and got an elbow up. BANG, right in his gob. The bus

85

went Brazilian, and my body had wrung its adrenaline makers. I ran hard ahead, and checked my shoulder, but the Englishman wasn't chasing. He was bent nearly double, face in his hands. I nearly went back to tell him sorry, but something stronger sent me on.

Here came the bus.

It passed me, doors closed.

Out an open window came a curly head. It was him with the T-shirt, *I spit left*. He gave a thumbs up, and said,

Fuckin eh!

I tried shouting *Stop*, but my voice was tiny.

The bus became a speck. I was out here alone.

———

The world disappeared. I disappeared.

Became an It.

It didn't think. It didn't run.

All It did was just not stop.

One It foot in front of the next.

———

He was big, noseguard big, a wide wet V on his brown T-shirt, brown shorts too, and (I looked twice) a pair of North Stars. Heavy pronation. The face on him red as Ragu and round.

Hi, he said

Hi.

We the last?

There was a bus.

Limey prick.

He tried to grab me.

I saw that. Nice move.

What if he comes back?

Countin on you to whup him.

What if he brings cops?

I'll tell 'em he assaulted you. Then sue his bony ass.

You're a lawyer?

Don't hold it against me.

You look like you play football.

I eat too many crullers. Christ, this is hard.

How many miles left, you think?

Five, more or less.

They took away the water.

Let's not stress the negative. What's your name?

I told him. What's yours?

Casey.

We knocked the backs of our hands together, his left hand, my right hand, and we kept on plodding. His thick upper legs along the inside were purple-red and bleeding.

———

Still with me?

Yeah.

Where you from?

Glanisburgh.

I know that town.

Pretty small.

The park.

Harris?

He nodded. Camped there once.

My Dad and me do hills in it.

He in this?

I nodded ahead. Finished now.

Nice to have someone there at the end.

I said, Casey?

He said, Yeah.

I don't know if I'll make it.

Wanna stop?

No.

OK then.

———

Ready? he asked.

You, I said.

Jeremiah. Was. Bullfrog.

Was. Good friend. Mine.
Never un'stood.
Word. He said.
Helped him.
Drink. His wine.
Always had.
Mighty. Fine wine.

We forgot the second verse, but kept on with the chorus, doing what we could with the breath we had.

———

Queen's Quay. Downtown was on our right. There were no more spectators, and nothing to mark the route.

Casey.

His head was lolling.

Casey. Where do we turn?

He could hardly point.

Spadina? I said.

He nodded.

The hill ahead was short but steep. Casey waved me on.

No, I said.

Can't, he said.

Casey, look at me. You have to breathe. *Look* at me.

I showed him how, the wrists.

Do it, I said. *Do* it.

OK.

Head *up*.

OK.

We crested the hill. He pointed right. The CN Tower. A small, dry sound escaped me.

———

No banner said FINISH. They had taken it down. The marshals had gone, the spectators. There was a line, but I ran past it, just to be sure.

Denny said, It's over, son.

I wasn't proud. I didn't care. Dad had been filming the last

88

50 yards. Casey told me, Go.

I pulled away from him.

He said, I'll be the one with bragging rights. Ran the Toronto Marathon. Finished absolutely last.

————

Dad and Denny took an arm each, and helped me up the stoop. Aunty Ag gaped.

God in Heaven, son. What have they done to ye?

Away she went and had a wee greet. I gagged down electrolytes, then filled the glass with plain cold water, and took it to the washroom, where Dad was slooshing Epsom salts all around the tub.

Give that a try.

Can't lift my leg.

Sit on the edge?

I tried, but could hardly bend my knees.

Right, he said. Togs off.

It embarrassed me some. My pubic hair. He pretended not to notice.

Put your arm around my neck. One, two, *hup*. Gaw you're an awful size.

He had run a marathon in three and one half hours, but he held me, and he tilted me.

Stick your toe in. Is it too hot?

I shook my head.

He stood me in the water, and took hold of my wrists.

Lean back, he said. Go on.

Bit by bit, he lowered me in. Stripped, and got in with me. Top to bottom and back again, he massaged my legs. I dunked my head, and lathered with Breck.

————

The inside of the *Herald* building smelt like ditto fluid. A man in an apron sent me upstairs. There was only one reporter. He was on the phone, taking notes in shorthand. An autographed photo of Stan Mikita was on the wall above his desk. Pens and pencils in a mug. An IBM electric. He thanked the Reeve very much for his time, then hung up.

Arsewipe.

Lit a Number 7, and swivelled in his chair.

You the marathon?

Yes, I said.

Have a seat.

The story when it came out was in a box in Sports, smaller than times-table flashcards. He put in how before the race my furthest run was fifteen miles, but nothing else of what I said. Vind is bitch. Three Dog Night. That woman in purple shorts.

Low Tide
Kathy Page

It was hot, the sky a bowl of blue; waves slapped against the rock. I remember still the astounding sensation of the air on my face, stomach, shoulders, back and limbs—all over, like invisible hands. How it was to stand upright on new legs and feet: utterly strange, yet easy, and then, a moment later, such a feeling of weight! The land's pull made each step an intentional thing and turned mere standing into an act of resistance. Intensely aware of my new flesh, I waded ashore and walked along the beach, leaving my prints in damp, newly exposed sand: my heels, the balls of my feet, my ten toes.

At the far end of the bay was a small island and a white and red lighthouse. A row boat had been dragged up on the beach and by the boat stood a man, watching me through binoculars. Did his watching change me that first time? Or did I, wet-dreaming until I caught fire, invent him, then split my pelt with longing and climb out of it? Maybe it was both of these things; in any case, at the beginning neither of us cared. When I drew closer, I noticed his clothes: long pants, a shirt, a jacket, all of them faded by the sun and ruffled by the breeze. Thinking that I might yet need my old sleek skin, I looked back then to the rocks, but the tide had turned and they were all but submerged. For a moment then I felt the sharpness of the sand blown in the breeze, and knew that the sun could burn me. And I missed my kind, the underwater sounds, all the old freedoms, but I told myself: *No matter, you must go on now*, and walked toward the man, who let the binoculars hang about his neck and strode, then ran to meet me.

His beard and hair were a mid brown, wiry, trimmed, if

roughly so. I liked his face. It broke open and contradicted itself:
he smiled, yet his cheeks were wet, his eyes, sea-green, wide with
astonishment.

"I knew you must come back!" He gasped for breath, his hands
heavy on my shoulders. "But not like this! Where the hell are
your clothes?" He laughed, sloughed his jacket, held it out for
me, though I did not feel embarrassed, despite the way his gaze
exposed me even as I covered myself. I noticed his skin glistened
with sweat. Would mine do the same?

"I've come from the sea," I told him, "I left my coat on the
rock." My voice emerged rough-edged, sore. He raised the binoculars again. "I think I see something dark in the water. We'll
take the boat and look."

So we pushed out. He took the oars and I the glasses, and I
quickly learned how to use them to bring the distance close. At
times I too thought I could see a dark thing floating just below
the surface of the water, but once we drew close I understood
that it was nothing but a reflection of the rock, and despite him
saying that whatever I had left there would likely wash up on
the shore, I knew that I must act as if my old skin was gone, and
that now I must live on land.

He said he was my *husband*. He kept the lighthouse, and as
well as that, he was a kind of artist, one who used science in the
service of beauty, he said. Surely I remembered that? And the
bed he had built for us on the third floor of the tower? Our wedding day, the drunken priest? The night of the storm?

"I remember none of it," I told him. I was sitting on a pile of
sacks in the stern of the boat. The ocean was flat and glossy, as
the tide flowed in and bit by bit filled up the bay it rippled
gently, as if there were muscles beneath its skin. Reflected light
flickered on our faces. The man who claimed to have married me
looked away a moment, then back.

"That may be for the best," he said. "Everything will be better
this time, Marina, I promise you. I'm very sorry. I think I had
every right to be angry, but I never meant to hurt you."

Naturally, I marked the word, *hurt*. And yet I knew that it
was not me that he spoke of, and he seemed sincere. I liked his
smoothness, the lean, muscular look of him, his strong-fingered
hands, the intensity of his gaze. And that first time, constrained

as we were by oars shelved to each side of us and by the struts and seats but most of all by being in a small vessel floating on the roof of my former world, can only be called exquisite: sex so gentle in its beginnings, so constrained and restrained—yet only seeming so, for within those limits our bodies' sensations were amplified like voices trapped in a cave, and at the end, shuddering, we broke free of all bounds, left the world and returned to it as if new. I saw, afterwards, that his hand bled from where he had slipped it between me and the floor of the boat.

Marina, he called me, yet he never thought to introduce himself, and I discovered his name only after he had taught me to read. From the start, he taught me a great deal. That first day he showed me how to manage the oars and it was I who pulled us back to the lighthouse island, along the narrow cove to the one place where it was possible, at certain times of day, to land. Together we hauled the boat beyond the tidemark and secured it with rocks. "You can walk around the island in an hour," he told me. By then, he had stopped saying that surely I remembered, and simply explained how things were and would be, though he frequently grasped my hand, as if to be sure that I was real.

He showed me a vegetable garden, a garden shed, a chicken coop, a smoke hut. The keeper's cottage, low with thick walls and small windows, was built right up against the tower. A smaller dwelling closer to the garden stood empty: out of parsimony, he said, the Lighthouse Board had not yet replaced the deputy keeper. His face darkened and he added that it was all the same to him, and likely they never would.... "In any case," he told me, gesturing at the tower, "the deputy is an unnecessary position now that my gearing system has so much improved the efficiency of the clockwork. The winding schedule is very manageable. You'll see."

In the future, he told me, all lighthouses would be powered by electricity, a thing like lightning, controlled. And they would be connected by another system of wires that carried voices from place to place and even from one continent to another.... But the very remotest of them, such as East Point, would likely wait until last. "And so until then," he said, pushing open the door into the kitchen, which was shady now but still warm from the range on the far wall, "we'll live here and be the world to each other." He pulled me close and reached under the jacket to feel the slippery heat between my legs. His hands shook as he unfastened the horn buttons, and soon we made good use of the table.

How willing I was! He liked that. Likewise, I told him, and he liked that, too. Both of us were greedy for pleasure. But more than that, I craved the deep forgetting at the heart of the act of love, that shedding of the trivial particulars that separate one being, one species, from another. Our desires were attuned, our bodies spoke. He fitted me. I liked him, from the length and firmness of what he called his member to the gleam of his body hair in the firelight and the long muscles of his arms and legs. He seemed a good mate, even though after the act he must ask, whispering, his lips to my ear, his hands restless on my skin,

"Did you open yourself like this to *him*? Even if you did so, I do forgive you, because you have returned. But tell me, please."

"I don't understand," I said and pulled away.

Afterwards I was always raging hungry, but I knew nothing of cooking and kitchens. This too I learned, though only to a degree: I kept my taste for raw things, and ours was a poor diet apart from the fish, mussels, and eggs. We had carrots, potatoes, cabbage and dill. Flour-and-water biscuits. Bitter coffee. Dried beans to be soaked in the pot. Ham. Salted butter and even saltier meats in cans. We frequently needed some brandy to wash down our meal.

And neither could I sew, and I saw no reason to. The machinery of the light interested me more. Above us, burning always, was the enormous light, reached by a long spiral climb that felt to me as if I was ascending inside a giant shell. The four oil lamps at the top of the tower were set inside a first order Fresnel lens taller than a man, a glass beehive, he called it, though also, I thought, it could be an gigantic insect eye. In daytime, the lens glittered and took on the colours of the sea and sky; at night its many planes glowed, so that it appeared to hover in the room: a hallucinatory vessel, a ship that might have travelled from beyond the moon. There were eight bull's-eyes to magnify the light. Above and below each of these were the panels set with many glass pieces. Each of these 944 curved sections had been individually cut and ground and then set exact in its curved brass mount. Light, like the sea, was made of waves, he said, and these glass prisms caught and focussed waves into a narrow, concentrated beam that could be seen twenty miles out to sea. Floating on mercury and driven by elaborate clockwork, the lamps revolved inside the lens, giving the beam its characteristic pulse.

Despite the ceiling ventilation it was unbearably hot near the light. Below, in the watch-room, it was cooler, and there, at five in the morning and five in the afternoon, without fail, we refilled the kerosene, and wound the clockwork tight. It was a circular room, with strong oak floors to support all our supplies and equipment, and generous windows all around to let in light. There was a desk, where the lighthouse records were written, and shelves where they were kept; a narrow door led out to the observation platform. The platform was also used to support the ladder when the light-room windows were cleaned after heavy storms, and in any case, according to regulation, no less than four times a year. Also in the watch-room was a bed built out from the wall: Why, he said, add in a journey up and down the spiral stairs when night observations needed to be taken. And why be separated? Why stay down in the gloom of the cottage, when there was so much light to be had and we could see each other so very well?

"I shouldn't believe in you," he said, looking up into my face while I knelt astride him on that bed, rocking and squeezing just enough to keep us both on the brink of our double descent, "but I must."

I always believed in him. But at night my underwater dreams seemed just as true: the dives and twists, the impossible grace and freedom of a lost world. More than once I woke in tears and the feeling lasted for days: a terrible grief and longing to be where I could no longer survive. All I could do then was gaze out to sea, or walk the shore cursing myself for being careless; I yearned for that dense, oily fur, the fat-sheathed musculature beneath. There was no remedy. But if he was gentle, he could ease me back to the pleasures of our life on the island off East Point, where gulls and terns and albatrosses soared and wheeled and plummeted into the water, and the wind blew clean and constant, bending the low grasses and the wild flowers and the few small trees back toward the mainland, and bringing with it the smells of ozone and kelp and emptiness, while all the time the clouds it pushed across the sky stretched and grew and shrank and grew again.

Still surrounded by the sea, I lived on land, a wife of sorts. I practised my letters. I learned how to keep the record. In a single sentence that ran across the width of the book I must include the weather, any passing vessels, any incidents, and the state of the equipment and supplies. I learned about the winds and Mr Howard's names for the clouds: the veils of cirrostratus, the ominous mounds of cumulonimbus, heavy with rain. I learned how to trim the lamps and clean the parts of the lens, how to use the telescope, how to calculate distance, read a chart and judge the course of a ship.

He did explain the camera, yet would not teach me to use it: the apparatus and the process were still in development, he said, the chemicals noxious.... More than that, I think, its power was new and excited him to a point that he could not bear to share it. He believed the camera would eventually be able to capture even the subtlest effects of the weather on the sea, and motion itself, but for now, the subject must remain still for minutes on end while the light worked its transformation on the plate. He could not have enough portraits: I posed both with and without clothes, standing, sitting and lolling on the rocks, in the water walking the beach, on the bed; I posed even while I slept, and was later able to see how soft and peaceful my face appeared when my eyes were closed.

He had a chest of clothing that he said was mine. *All right!* A woman's, at least, he said. Though why? I was comfortable enough in his shirts.

"Just try them," he said. "I want to see." We rifled through and I marvelled at the vast skirts, a boned bodice, at the tiny mother or pearl buttons on the placket and sleeves of elaborate shirts pattered with tiny flowers and needle-fine stripes. Everything but the skirts and bloomers looked too small. But the rustle of it all! Such stuff! I tied the corset around my head with a shirt, pulled a pair of drawers over his.

"Like this?"

"Though of course," he said once our laughter subsided, "this is what you will have to wear when Mr Davis visits to make the inspection at the end of the month."

"Really?" I told him, wiping my eyes. "You'll have to show me how."

He reached into the chest and pulled out two small shapeless pieces of fabric.

"For your legs," he explained. "Would you please just try them?"

The material, I later learned, was made from moth cocoons and the finest, water-repellent wool of a special breed of sheep; all clothes then were made from beasts and plants. And the stockings did settle lightly on my skin, almost but not quite as if they were part of me. Serious, then, he fetched his camera, set up the stand, then posed me on the bed all but nude, propped up on my elbows, legs akimbo, in such a way that any viewer's gaze would follow the dark lines of my stockinged legs to where my sex, part anemone, part oyster, stretched between the two white strips of upper thigh.

"Don't blink. Stay still," he warned me, the watch ticking in his hand.

And after that, there were yet more photographs. These light pictures, he told me, made by and of the real body, were no mere daubs or imitations or interpretations, but a physical print of sex itself—that raw thing that joined humankind to the beasts, the irrational heart in the thinking machine, the greedy void that hid beneath the skirts of romance, the thing that lodged not just between our legs but also somewhere deep in the brain, hidden in a place that would some day be found and understood.... The century to come, he told me, would be all about seeing the invisible, the interiors of our bodies and minds, the atoms of matter, the surfaces of the moon and stars. Open your legs wider, he said. Touch yourself.

And after all, he decided, it was far better that the inspector did not see me. Let alone the challenge of dressing—her things, whoever she was, did not fit me, a woman still part wild—his neglect in reporting my return would involve too much explanation. The smoke-house was the obvious place for me to hide during the inspection. But it was always possible that just this once Mr Davis would decide to glance in there, or that I might grow restless, peer out of the window as they passed and give us both away.... Did I understand how important discretion was?

Not really, no. Not yet. Any suspicions I had floated too deep to see or really feel; I knew only that something new burned inside him and that I disliked it.

Suppose I waited the visit out in the bay at the north end? The inspector would never go there, would not even know such a private spot existed. Or better still, leave me on the mainland—I'd shelter in a cave or bush until it was safe to return.... I do believe the keeper saw the sense of these stratagems, and even wanted to enact them. But he could not. He could not allow me to be beyond his sight and reach.

"Why ask," I said, "if you will not hear what I say?" He caught me by the arm as I turned away; I bit him, drew blood. We fought hard, breathed in grunts as we yanked and twisted, gasping at what the other could inflict: though either we were perfectly matched, or neither of us was quite prepared to deliver defeat. Our struggle took us to the ground, and there turned blow by blow into its opposite, or else love became a battle; it's hard to say which, and when we woke, bruised and aching in the half light of a new morning we were shocked at ourselves, terrified, when realised that we had slept, fucked or fought through the changing of the lamps. A strong wind buffeted the tower and though there was no sign of any harm done, we might never know if someone had been misled by the darkness.

We were both over-wrought, he said, and offered a tonic: another of his inventions. Just a few drops on the tongue—a sweetness, which soon became metallic. Then a vast, dense fog surrounded and infiltrated me, overwhelmed all my senses, first sight, then hearing, touch, and smell. I slept so soundly that I could neither move or cough, but for good measure he tied me and fit me inside a box: I know this only because of the photograph. And shortly after I came to in the watch-room, weak, hungry and at the same time nauseated, the birth pangs began to roll through my lower belly and up the insides of my thighs.

He would not seek help. There *was* none, he said.

Limbless, covered in thick fur, her small face arranged around dark, deep eyes like mine, our child was still born. I wrapped her and held her close, knew I must return her to the sea, and begged him to let me go down to the rocks. "I'll take you," he said, and though his voice was gentle, he was rightly fearful that I might swim away or drown myself. He grasped my hand tight and would not let go as we clambered back from the waster's edge.

And perhaps it was to the good, he said, adding syrup and a measure of brandy into hot tea: the same for each of us, and I watched him drink first. The island was no place for a child, he said. Mere breeding was not what free thinkers such as he and I were for.

Free?

He said that he understood that I was sad, that words failed me, but he knew it would pass. And luckily, we had our work for the light, the routine around which all else must be fitted.... Winter would come soon, bringing storms. We must eat well, gather back our strength, and put everything in order.

Now he wore the keys at his waist and locked doors behind him. When he was away, I was bound to the bed. And I yet I also worked my share, cleaning the panels of the lens, and, when permitted on the windy platform outside the watch-room, I scanned the sea for ships. I explored my prison too; I found, folded and tucked into the back of the bible an article headlined *Tragic Death at East Point*: Two days after the storm of 3 November, it reported, the battered body of the deputy light keeper at East Point had been found washed up some three miles south of the island, following a failed attempt to launch the lightship craft in order to aid a whaler in distress. The fate of the whaler was still unknown.

A small key at the back of the desk drawer led me to a box containing a single photographic print of a woman who could only be my namesake: she wore the clothes I had handled, and stood against the whitewashed cottage wall, her blond hair blurring in the breeze. Beneath the photograph was a lock of red-gold hair, and a copy of the signed statement the keeper had submitted the day following the discovery of his colleague's body. *I was sadly mistaken*, he wrote, *in thinking my poor wife cured of an*

99

infirmity for which she had in the past been treated. Acting impulsively during a fit of hysterical mania brought on by the storm and feelings of guilt concerning the loss of the deputy, she cast herself into the water while I slept.

And now the days shortened; flocks of birds passed, returning north across the vastness of the ocean. I said nothing to the keeper, but thought often of Marina, whose body had never been found. Had she loved the deputy keeper, or simply been the object of his affections? I did not like to think of her as drowned, let alone murdered. Did she go into the sea? Perhaps she was like me, but able to return? Had she found her skin? Or did she swim in the awkward human way to the mainland, and make some kind of escape.... Who knew, I told myself, but that she might be living with natives in the bush, or have got so far as the town and have booked her passage out under a new name. Out there on the platform, buffeted by the winds, I breathed in the cold salt air and watched the sea birds, marvelling at the way they stayed together, and at the steady beating of their wings, mile on mile. The largest birds, the mollymawks, pass without apparent movement or effort through the air; their wings fixed, just barely tilting from side to side to ride the currents like waves they simply turn their heads they way they wish to go.... Such huge birds, the mollies, yet it was as if they had no weight. I watched them slip and soar and it lifted my heart. I longed for the bird-feeling and imagined it: the ocean and the land spread out beneath in intricate detail, but also in depth and with extraordinary focus. In my mind's eye I saw, as if from very far above the rocks, the island and the tower where I myself stood looking out. The wind blew steadily to the east and the air seemed to offer itself to me. And I would not go back inside, would not endure another night with Clarence Morgan, the clockwork beneath us unwinding itself cog by cog until the next time it must be set, and the next, and the next. Ignoring his call, I climbed onto the rails, balanced for one terror-stricken moment then gave myself to the wind. Immediately I felt the new strength in my chest and back, the structural dominance of two great limbs.

The water below was almost pink. Just two wing-beats, and

I was rising fast. I could no longer hear his call, and did not look back, for the air is a kind of ecstasy, a far freer thing than even a swimmer could believe.

Yet I'll admit that come spring, on my way to the grounds, I did return, and landed on a low cliff to watch my former keeper, on the beach below, set up a new version of his camera. The apparatus was directed at the seals sunning themselves on the rocks. He was thinner and older than I recalled. He had broken his promise not to hurt me, and there was a gun slung over his shoulder that I knew he might use. Yet even so, watching him, I felt for the first time the need to open my wings wide and stretch my neck to its utmost, then tuck my head deep down this way, then that, to stretch and bow and tread out the steps of our dance. A sound came out of me, part shriek, part moan: oh, look at me! For looking is the beginning of the dance. He must see me exactly as I am and what I do, the exact way of it, and I likewise. And by scrupulous imitation, turn on turn, we come to see better and prove to each other that we see, and what we see. We must show that each can and will exactly follow the other, or, failing, try again.

Hearing me, the keeper turns and reaches for his binoculars. He faces me, but gives no sign of recognition or sympathy. My call dies in my throat; I put myself into the wind, run, and scull hard until the updraft bears me and I ride suddenly without effort, free of the earth's jealous pull; I soar above vast ocean into the even vaster air. I must fly on to the place where I will meet my kind, and find the one with whom I can perfect the dance.

The Dog and the Sheep
Cynthia Flood

Late in the afternoon the dog appeared again, around a curve some way ahead on the road.

She had often come trotting back to us. We were slow, halting often to name and photograph a flower, or to query as our tour guide spoke of local limestone formations. Of French cheese-making. Of the peasant houses (animals downstairs, people up) in the Cathar villages we'd visited. Of the Cathar heresy, whose adherents saw evil and good as equal powers, chose poverty, strove to be kind. Of their betrayers, informants paid in the usual currencies of cash or sex.

"Shocking," we agreed.

French wine-making, too. Terroir, very important.

Nearer the dog came, wagging, closer, until those at the front of our walking group cried out.

Others halted.

In a huddle, we all stared.

Blood covered the dog's muzzle, stained the delicate fur beneath her eyes, dabbled an ear.

"My God, what's she done?"

"Horrible!"

Our cries drove her off a little, puzzled, her tail drooping. Through that red mask she peered at us over her shoulder.

Early that morning, this dog had turned up.

As we left the gîte where we'd spent the night, we'd spoken of the Inquisition's unsparing work in that particular village. In 1308 every single resident got arrested for heresy.

Our walking tour itself was titled In The Footsteps of the Cathars, though most participants had signed up to see the beauty of the Pyrenean foothills. Some did feel that faith, if not extreme, might sustain social order? In a good way? One or two, confusing Cathars with Camino, had expected to follow a specific route taken by all the heretics to a singular destination.

"I wonder how many Cathars, total, got burned at the stake."

"Are we going to be so gloomy all day?"

"I'm just glad I didn't live then."

"Tomorrow's the castle of the Really Big Burn."

"Oh no, not rain again!"

Past the last house in the village, our guide paused till we all caught up. "Our way starts here."

We stood by a single gravestone at a field's edge, a stone tilting somewhat and obscured by long wet grass. Ici est morte, we read in our remembered high-school French, Ici est morte / 18 aout 1944 / Castella Pierre / innocente victime / de la barbarie Nazie.

"Glad I wasn't here for that, either."

Then this dog rose out of a ditch.

A mutt. Thin, scruffy, brown, collar-less, small-eyed. Dark long nipples swinging. She came close, wouldn't quite allow pats, whimpered, scuttled away, returned to circle and sniff, hung back till she saw where we tended. Then she rushed forward to wait for us, panting.

"D'you suppose she has puppies somewhere near?"

"Get away!" Our guide thrust his hazel stick at her. She yelped.

"If she has, she'll go back to the village," we concluded, and went on.

As we were led from one thin grassy path to another and then to a narrow road of beaten earth, light rain continued. On all sides now the fields spread out in their spring greens, shining wet, and in the distance the terrain sloped up, polka-dotted with sheep, to a forested plateau.

"Up there we shall walk," our guide said.

The dog trotted ahead, looking back to check we were still in view. The breeze wafted moisture at us, swirled it into loose airy necklaces.

Behind us sounded a—truck? French. So little!

We smiled, moving aside for the vehicle to pass, but it stopped so the three men inside could joke and talk with our guide. They spoke so fast we grasped nothing.

The driver pointed inquiringly at the dog.

"Problème." Our guide shrugged. More laughter.

As the van moved off, the unknown men wiggled their eyebrows at us and waved.

"Foresters," said our guide. "They work not far from where we walk today. To remove the rotten branch. Inspect for pasts, no, pests."

"But how on earth do they manage with that van? Trop petite!"

"Earth? Manage?"

The discussion lasted until we neared a larger road. In its middle sat the dog. Intently she watched us approach, her head sticking up above the hedge lining the route.

"Thinks she's hiding."

"Stupid! She'll get run over."

"Never been trained."

"Why the hell doesn't she go back where she came from?"

Our guide chased the dog until she howled and ran off.

"Good!"

We crossed the road and walked alongside a field. Its unknown tall grains swayed close by us, and their wet silky heads made moiré patterns under the breeze. Mesmerizing.

Without notice, our guide made a turn into a tall green tunnel of shrubs and small trees (in Ireland, a boreen) that ran off at an angle from the field. We'd not noticed the entrance, draped with wet vines.

"Just as well this isn't a self-guided tour!"

"Too right, we'd be lost in no time."

After emerging from the tunnel we started uphill, and half an hour later paused to look back at the valley we'd traversed. In the rain it formed a long trough full of silver-green air, resembling the great stone troughs in the ancient villages we'd passed through, shapes empty now but once alive, sparkling with laundry and the hands of women.

Now we were ascending a great staircase, up on what had once been terraced farmland. Disuse had blurred the steps to faint ledges.

The rain got serious. We stopped to put on rain-pants and

jackets, and went on.

After an hour the dog re-appeared, wagging madly. A hand reached out to pat. She snapped, cringed, ran.

"Damn that bitch!"

"Maybe her puppies got taken too early, and she's upset."

"Couldn't we get her back to where we started?"

"Are you kidding?"

Our guide, looking dour, moved on. We followed.

The temperature dropped steadily, the rain chilled. As hands went into pockets for gloves and woolly hats, the dog came near again. She'd stretch out her front paws and drop her head, abasing herself, and then look up in hope.

"No! Nothing for you."

We climbed. She came close, sniffed, almost nudged.

"Go home!" Whack of the hazel stick.

She yelped, but stuck around.

When at last we attained the forested plateau, the dog pranced about and shook herself as if happy to be in the dry at last. So were we. All of us were wrong. Up there, a freshening wind blew rain through the trees and also made their foliage shed thousands of cold drops already accumulated.

Our way was stony, muddy, and so narrow that the dog left the track to move to and fro among the trees. Some of us tried that too, but low branches and hidden roots made our balance as uncertain as did the stones underfoot. Stepped on, they often slid. We stepped in liquid mud, stepped, stepped among the black pines sheathed in ebony plates. Sweet-smelling fir. The thin grey trunks of fagus sylvatica. Holm oaks, festooned with catkins.

"Where's that dog got to?"

"Who cares?"

"Headed back to the village, probably."

"Sensible creature's gone to shelter. Not like us!"

Everyone laughed.

Not our guide. "A dog to run about the forest is not good. Higher up on the montaigne is wild boar. Deer. Sheep of course. And—wolfs?"

"Wolves."

We went on.

Were those animals observing us as we came through their country? Some in our group had seen wild boars on YouTube. Not as large as pigs. Mean tusks, though. One told a story from a TV newscast about a huge sow in Ontario stomping on a drunk, killing him.

A howl sounded from behind, a blundering rush. We turned. Just as the frantic dog reached us, we sensed a blurred motion away, away in the trees and gone, like a curtain shaken then still.

"Roe deer," said our guide. "Bad animal!" He shook his stick.

The dog's chest heaved. Whining, she skulked off, followed again.

Then the terrain altered.

Plateau, fini. We started downhill. That steepness—odd, to be almost vertical after two hours' walking on the flat! Our feet felt unfamiliar. The trees changed too. More conifers, fewer deciduous. Progress, we thought.

Also we wondered, Lunch? Daily, leaving our gîtes, we each got a bag holding ten inches of buttered baguette (we measured) stuffed with meat or fish plus hard-boiled egg and tomato. Local cheese, a slab. Cold meat, sliced. Fresh salad. Cake. Our guide carried dark chocolate, also a mini camp-stove for hot drinks.

We went on.

The rainy twist of trail down through the trees grew steep and steeper. We slowed, slowed. Many stones now underfoot were larger than those up on the plateau, but they still slipped. Terracotta-coloured mud ran two inches thick, clogging our boots. Our hiking poles must be used for every step, while our guide moved urgently amongst us to point out safe foot placements, to repeat Attention! Rain fell. Occasionally some of us did too, delaying the group to cope with minor injuries.

We murmured of forestry campsites at home, of fire-watchers' cabins. Did our guide plan a lunch-stop at a similar place?

The dog came close again, but whenever a hand reached out she'd show her teeth. Shouts and rushes drove her off, snarling.

Watch! Attention!

Always the path turned down through the pines to—where? None of us knew. With fewer deciduous trees, the forest's ambience dulled. No more wry jokes about la boue. Silence, except curses and rain.

Again the dog came close. On her forelegs, mud reached well above the carpal pad.

"Poor thing!"

"Poor thing bit me, remember?"

"She needs people."

"Well, we don't need her."

Another distant noise sounded, r-rr-rrrrrr. Not animal, mechanical. Piercing. It'd hurt your ears, close up. Rrr-r-r-r-r.

"Must be the foresters."

"Why haven't we seen them?"

Why indeed? What route had they taken? Surely that cartoon vehicle couldn't go cross-country like an ATV?

Then our guide loosened his pack. "Time to eat."

Here? Steep slope. Dripping pines. No stumps or rocks to sit on.

Standing in a ring of soggy backpacks on the forest floor, we ate.

R-rr-rrrr, further off.

The dog grovelled, whined, begged. Our guide, about to shoo her, aborted his gesture when one of us tossed her a slice of ham. Another threw torn bits of baguette on the mud. A tomato landed there, a cube of cheese, half a hard-boiled egg.

Even as the dog swallowed, her pleading glance moved up again.

"C'est tout!" Our guide raised his voice.

"No more for you, greedy girl."

Some of us ate all our lunch, some repacked much of it. We stretched, or leaned against trees to relax while drinking coffee and tea, well-sugared. The dog sidled amongst us, sniffing at hands, bums, packs.

"Are you deaf? That's all!"

Packs on again, poles in hand, la boue again.

Down those stony steeps for another nameless time, down, down.

More slips, delays, wrenches, bruises. We went on. Only the chill rain stayed steady, and the dog slinking off into the trees (who cared what kinds they were?) or weaving amongst us on her muddy paws. Once, close to the trail, she squatted.

"Dammit, not right here!"

Small dry turds.

How far, how much longer, when? Some asked, others cringed. Like kids pestering a parent, we knew what our guide would say.

Then the rain ceased. Unnoticed, for some moments. At ten that morning we'd reached the plateau; our watches said 5 PM when we realized that the sound of falling water was MIA.

The steep softened first into a hill, next to a gentle slope. The dog lolloped ahead, out of sight. In sunshine, peeling off sodden jackets and hats and gloves, we exited the forest laughing.

For the first time in hours, our guide smiled. "Now we see the Kermes oak. Not the holm any more."

Our legs, trembling, sought to adjust as we moved into the valley and across a sunny meadow sprinkled with primula, tricolour pansy, anemone, cowslip, speedwell—all bright-eyed still with rain.

The foothills rose ahead, one crowned with the grey ruined teeth of the castle where the greatest immolation had occurred. To be bundled alive into the flames or to deny their faith: two choices, those Cathars had.

We walked alongside a brook whose current carried a thousand spangles downstream, and soon reached a gravel road. This, our guide assured us, led to the nearby town where we would spend the night.

Round a curve ahead, the dog appeared again. Came closer, trotting, wagging. Those at the front of our group stopped.

We all stopped.

"Look, horrible!"

"Awful!"

"What's she done?"

Over her shoulder, that puzzled red face, peering.

We hastened forward.

In a depression at the roadside lay a large ewe, fallen.

She could nearly have been an illustration for a children's book, that sheep. Background: blue sky, tall green grass. Foreground: the beautiful creature in her seemingly restful motherly pose, in her roundness, her billowy shining creamy woolliness—but her swelling hindquarters, fully exposed to our view, had been savaged to a bloody mangle. One leg was raw. She could not move.

Patient, full of pain, her large eyes met our gaze.

"Wolf," stated our guide.

"Not—?"

"Her? No no, too stupid, she just sticks in her nose for a taste. Wolf." He pointed at the steeps we'd just descended.

Some loudly wished for a gun, a knife.

Others noted that the sheep was not ours to kill.

We walked on along the valley.

The brook, still shallow, grew broader. While fording it, by silent agreement we lured with ham the red-faced dog who'd chosen us. We grabbed her, struggling, yelping, to splash and rub her furry face till she no longer looked a murderer. While controlling her thus, we touched her nipples. Hard as horn. No loved puppies, not for years.

At the first farm we came to, our guide went in to leave word of the desperate sheep, so that her owner in this life could be notified and come to end his property's pain.

"They will phone him," he said, returning.

Would this happen before the wolf came back?

We went on.

The dog circled near, ran off, came back. No-one threw food. No-one tried to pat. Why, we asked ourselves, did this animal, so obviously fearing yet desiring human contact, not have a home?

Did the SPCA operate in France? Even if so, there'd hardly be a branch in the small town.

Why are people so careless?

Why do they not train their dogs?

Why do they not affix identification tags to their dogs' collars, vaccinate the animals, have their teeth checked?

What could we do about the damn dog?

"La mairie," said our guide when we put the matter to him. "We'll take her there."

The town hall was closed, though, by the time we'd walked over the centuries-old bridge (our stream had grown to a river) and threaded our way along the narrow streets, faced with houses washed in white or cream, to the green of the central square. Here stood rubbish bins where we dumped our leftovers, and here a fountain played near a large memorial to locals killed in one or another World War. A smaller, special stone was dedicated to local héros de la résistance. The plane trees' dappled trunks were re-dappled by the late sun among the leaves, and, on one corner of the square, red shutters shielded the windows of our small hotel.

Exhaustion, held back for hours, at this sight filled all of us. We entered the lobby, the dog pushing forward too.

"Mais non," said Monsieur to the animal that had walked twenty kilometres with us that day. (Perhaps 30, given how she'd run back and forth and circled?) The door, closing, touched her nose.

Later we came down to a pleasant sitting-room that looked out through small panes to the hotel's courtyard, bright with red pelargoniums. A fire warmed the hearth. Madame, smiling, poured kir for us and for guests from other tours. Quite a United Nations we made, really, travellers from every continent.

And here were the foresters again. One exclaimed, "You made so loud noise!" All three laughed. Graceless, we felt. Dumb tourists, trailed unawares by savvy locals.

Another forester chortled, "We found this." A glove, with a clip for attaching to a belt. "Not latched, no good! This, too." A candy wrapper.

Barbarians.

The third commented, "That dog with you, we see her often today. No good in the woods. No sense."

"Ouaf ouaf, all the time!" agreed Monsieur. "I have let her stay there," and he pointed to the courtyard, "tonight. Then she goes out."

A wicker chair beside a puddle offered partial shelter from the rain. Nose on paws, the bitch looked up.

"Out where?"

Monsieur made the face that says Not my concern. No, his busy schedule wouldn't feature escorting a stray to the town hall. As for Madame, her mien indicated complete abstention from this topic.

"Couldn't we—?"

Our guide answered, "We leave too early."

After a jagged silence, one forester suggested that he and his fellows return the dog to the village we'd walked from, that day.

"We work there tomorrow. It is her home, yes?"

Who knew?

The glove's owner pocketed it, while Monsieur tossed the crumpled candy wrapper on to the flames. Its silvery coating flared. We all sipped kir.

A South African exclaimed, "Dinner smells wonderful, Madame!"

A Scot agreed, and a Californian. We all agreed.

While we were at table, Monsieur talked about the magnificent trees on the terrain we'd crossed. Especially he admired the strength and longevity of the Kermes oak. In calcareous, pebbly soil it throve, indifferent to that chemistry.

We asked him about the semi-deserted villages we'd walked through, the proliferating À Louer and À Vendre signs, the shut schools, the ancient churchyards poorly maintained.

He considered. "Every century has its disasters. These are ours."

Madame nodded. We went on to her hazelnut cake.

All night it rained.

Next day's breakfast featured blackcurrant and apricot jams, made by la maman et la belle-maman de Madame from fruit grown in the hotel's garden. Croissants, home-made. We ate quite fresh oranges. The foresters were not at table, nor the dog in the courtyard.

Soon the tour company's van arrived, to take us to the start of our climb to the site of the great burning. We looked forward to being driven. Our luggage stuffed in, we squeezed giggling on to the narrow seats as our hosts bade us a courteous farewell.

In another town at the end of that day we ate a celebratory dinner to conclude the tour, laughing, talking, at a table crowded with bottles and cell-phones and serving dishes. As we finished the wine, some of our group confessed that at dawn they'd heard barking. Had opened the red shutters to witness the dog's struggle, see the men bundle her into the funny truck and take her away.

Where to?

That query segued into Where next?

One was due at the airport by 7 AM for a Munich flight, one

for Amsterdam. Sure, share a taxi. Brilliant signage, these European airports had. A Danube cruise, old pals in Barcelona, a family reunion in Edinburgh—happy plans, though It'll be good to get home won several repeats.

Best then to wrap up the evening now, finish packing. Bustle of bill and tip, purses closing, wallets folded. That beautiful sheep—we spoke of her too. Her great shining eyes, what colour? Some of us thought dark blue, some remembered brown.

Rhubarb
Lauren Carter

Josie's family came from Saudi Arabia when we were in Grade 4. She stood at the front of class as the teacher introduced her, one hand cupping a bony elbow and the ends of her long hair tangled like they'd been dipped in sugar. We watched as she, alone in the schoolyard, wound her fingers through the chain-link and stared out at the lake, at the fishery's squat white boats motoring out and back in, seagulls accompanying them like kites. I wondered what it was like moving somewhere with so much water after a place with so much sand but I didn't ask her or say anything about it to Sam and Lara as we whispered in a clutch by the gym door, beside the four-square. Over the weeks Josie's colour faded to a tan and she became one of us, her pigtails jumping in the blur of plastic pink rope.

When you're a teenager, you never want to think it, but by Grade 10 I pretty much figured we'd drift apart. Even though Sam talked about us having babies, renting summer cottages so our husbands could go fishing at dawn. "But Bruce Cartwright?" Lara would say when we were seventeen, and it was obvious it wouldn't work. Lara, with her nose ring and dragonfly tattoos, was out of place in that fantasy—the fridge chattering with beer bottles, the guys barbequing bloody steaks while we did the dishes and handed out fruit-juice Popsicles to the kids.

Right after high school, Josie married Bruce Cartwright. The wedding was okay but Samantha, Lara, and I sat at our table in shock. We were headed for university and here was Josie, Bruce burrowing under her lace-and-polyester dress for the garter belt in the room above the hockey rink. Fake purple lilacs on the tables. Peas and carrots, mashed potatoes, turkey drying out in the chafing dishes.

Josie's parents paid for the wedding because they had money. We all knew that. Her dad worked at the uranium refinery and her mother was a home nurse. When they moved to town, they bought one of the new houses, half brick, half siding, on Concession Road. During the spring and summer, Lara and I would walk by sometimes but we never dropped in unless we were invited. One summer Josie's mother planted a vegetable garden in the front yard but we didn't see her outside, not once, and soon it was all a weed-clenched shambles, deflated orange tomatoes glowing on the lawn.

On the upstairs level of the market, Josie finishes her coffee and sets the empty mug on another table so the busboy can pick it up. I've still got most of mine because I like to drink it slow. I hold it with both hands while she picks at her half of a Texas donut, eating like a bird, choking down each crumb. With her free hand she plays with my car keys, with the peacock feather key chain Lara sent me for my last birthday when I turned 32. Other than on Facebook, no-one else remembered although I didn't really expect to hear anything from Sam.

I drove today, because Jo's car is on the fritz, a busted alternator she told me about on the way over, when she met me after school and we drove downtown. Now she's got this look on her face like the hard chocolate icing is way too sweet and I'm waiting for her to confess whatever's bothering her but she keeps talking about the house.

"There were tons of cops there," she says, meaning last August, a month before I moved back. A whole winter's passed since and now the leaves are coloured that new neon green of spring. "The driveway was all clotted up with vehicles," Josie says. "Jammed in like a used car lot."

She tried to get a good shot of the HazMat team coming out of the lab but there were too many details crowded into her lens. When she moved, stepping backwards, the leaves of a gigantic rhubarb brushed against her bare calves. "Biggest I've ever seen," she says. Her spoon stabs the air between us, punctuating the thought. "It takes years to get that big. Decades."

Except for the part about the plant, I already know most of

what she's saying from living in a small town but I let Josie talk. She's the expert. She's the one who writes articles for the local paper, stood on the road that summer day with her camera and took pictures of an officer hauling a man wearing studded leather pants and a red wife-beater through the front door. Arms behind his back, wrists bound by a plastic zip-tie. When they let her on the property, the officers posed beside a pool table, its torn green felt heaped with guns, and then escorted her into the Quonset hut so she could see the beakers, stripped batteries, residue-stained mason jars for herself.

That house has always been bad news but when we were teenagers it was fun. The Donnelly family owned it. My mother, an English teacher at the Catholic high school, called them the Black Donnellys because the parents relocated to the Yukon for work and left the place in the hands of their sixteen- and eight-een-year-old kids. Every weekend there were parties. The cops were always showing up. Once Lara rolled out a bedroom window and broke her wrist before the police could bust in and charge her with underage drinking. Usually I sat on the garage roof with the others, sipping from a communal bottle of cherry whisky or lemon gin while we invented dialogue for films play-ing at the drive-in theatre across the field. Sometimes we'd watch in silence, aware of the prickle of heat between our knees as the giants kissed. We all wanted that, especially those of us on the garage roof and not in the back bedroom before the waterbed broke or downstairs on the basement couch. Those characters found love while we lined the rooftop like ravens, looking for something shiny to steal. In the years between then and now: biker gangs, drug busts, city hookers haunting the doorway at 3 AM. Everything's changed.

"It's such a waste," Josie says, licking chocolate off her fingertip, and I think of her mother's old garden: spiky arugula gone to seed, zucchinis swelling into oblong balloons, woody, not worth harvesting. "Tomorrow's Saturday," she tells me.

My spare-room is still full of boxes and I was planning to spend the day unpacking, although I know what that means: that I'm staying, settling in, attempting to co-exist with the awkward shadow of my youth. It's sticky, that shadow. Everywhere I go it fastens to me, like a piece of toilet paper dragging on my heel. I shift in my seat.

"Why didn't you get it right then? Ask to dig it up and bring it home?"

She shrugs one shoulder in that exaggerated way, a forward roll like her muscles are aching and she's trying to stretch them out. Her body curves around her centre. "They wouldn't let me. Then winter came and I kept thinking about it." She spreads her left hand on the table. "I guess it's stupid," she says, staring at the miniature glitter of her ring.

I swallow the last sweet treacle of my double-double and don't respond. Josie usually needs reassurance but I've never heard her talk like this: so sad about something that seems so small. Her voice is whiny when it comes again.

"Now Bruce says I can't use the truck."

"Asshole," I mutter.

Josie looks up. "People don't realize how stressful it is to be an electrician." When I don't respond she pushes the last of her donut away and asks me if I want to see a movie, a remake of the Jungle Book playing at the theatre downtown. I don't want to. It's a kids' movie and I know how it will be: the theatre overrun with adolescents on dates, calling across the audience, their sneakers suctioning to the sticky floor as they run up and down the aisles. That's what it was like for us: popcorn thrown over the heads of adults who didn't realize the place was ours.

"What are you doing there?" Lara asks me on the phone that night. I'm drunk on a single bottle of wine, sitting on the cold cracked tile of the bathroom floor. I shove a hand into my hair, hold it back from my face.

"Where are you?" I ask.

"At home." I hear her smoking, the inhale and exhalation, and imagine her analyzing one of her paintings, figuring out what colour it needs as smoke curls against the ceiling.

I always thought I was right behind her, that I'd send Josie a few e-mails from university, stay friends with her on Facebook, but that my experiences would be too thrilling for her to understand. Life is funny though. University led to teachers' college to several years supply teaching in the city before I finally got a

116

contract teaching Grade 5. It happened to be back home. My parents aren't here anymore—they moved south after my sister left for college—so Josie let me stay with her and Bruce before I found my own place. He was okay, but unpredictable, either cracking jokes or so withdrawn it seemed he was only half there. One night he backhanded a bowl of olives across the kitchen. Purplish brine all over the wall, a spackling of red pepper flakes.

"I don't remember him like that," I said to Josie that night, after he left, trying to comfort her. In Grade 10, drunk, Bruce had kissed Lara during the last song of the Hawaiian dance and then refused to talk to her the next day when she called him. The summer before Grade 12 he and Josie hooked up at a house party and she slept with him on a trampoline in the backyard. Afterward, they lay there for a long time, affecting each other with their smallest movements. It sounded romantic to me back then but I always remembered Lara rolling her eyes.

I see he's still a jerk, Lara wrote back when I told her about the olives in a text.

"Seriously, Mel," she says now.

My voice gurgles up. "I don't have a choice. Go where the work is. Do you know how hard it is to find a contract?"

"Yeah, yeah."

Probably she's right. I could have gone anywhere—a fly-in reserve in Northern Manitoba, England, maybe even Saudi Arabia. "I don't know," I say, and at that moment the train whistle blows, a lonely siren north of town. It's the sound that punctuated our childhood.

"Hear that?"

"Yeah," she says. "It just gave me the heebie-jeebies."

"Why don't you come for a visit?" I ask like I do almost every time. She doesn't say no, but I hear the groan of distance, 500 kilometres of forest and lakes and the rock of the Canadian Shield squeezing between our words.

The house is a split level with grubby yellow siding covered in scrawls of red graffiti: *guvernmint off our land, cops r pigs*. Dead yellow grass clots the front yard. The abandoned Toyota that kids used to make out in sits beside the dirt driveway, hood popped, and I can't believe it's still there. Years marked by a fringe of crumbling rust on the wheel wells, the web of the shattered windshield.

It's dusk, nearly dark, and we've driven in over the collapsed yellow crime scene tape. The investigation into the biker gang is ongoing, Josie's told me, although they just get the stories from the wire service now so she no longer has the inside scoop. It's old history. We're trespassing, I know that much, but Josie doesn't seem to care. I haven't seen her so bold in years although I know she'd never be here if I hadn't agreed to come. Sleeping with Bruce at that party was probably the most daring thing she's ever done.

We park facing the Quonset hut. "Was that even there then?" I ask.

"That's where Luke built his model airplanes."

The older brother. The hum of a WWII replica bomber diving into a circle of smoking teenagers. "Who'd ever heard of meth back then," Josie says, as she opens the car door, but I remember plenty of cocaine, miniature ridges piling up on math and science textbooks, fat novels for English class like *Fifth Business* and *A Canticle for Leibowitz*.

My flashlight jumps over the ground, shines on the silver chain-link fence that the bikers installed. When Josie shouts, *there*, I have to reverse direction and follow her pointing finger with the beam. She squats down, brushes the earth with her searching fingers, and looks up at me, smiling.

The rhubarb seems impossibly young. Tiny wizened leaves that look like brains, stalks sprouting from a tissuey pocket that's fleshy and pink. Against the dun-coloured earth the plant is vibrant red, like part of a human pushing out of the ground. We crouch on either side. Josie strokes the edge of the small, bumpy leaves. "I thought you said it was big," I say.

"They die away over winter."

I'm surprised by her knowledge. I'm not a gardener myself and her mother seemed to fail miserably. We're ready with the cardboard box and the spade and really I just want to get moving. I'd spent the afternoon unpacking things I realized I could have lived without and felt tired.

Josie stabs the shovel into the ground. She tries to lift the whole thing but the plant tugs against her. "Huge root system," she says, and starts again, piercing the blade deeper until she can scoop it all out: a bucket-sized clump of earth and those red stalks, almost unrecognizable as a plant, a thing that will actually grow.

When we slide it into the trunk of my car, Josie lays the spade down and says, "What now?"

"You should get that in the ground."

"Don't you want to see what's playing?"

Across the field, the screen of the drive-in movie theatre is darker than the surrounding sky. It shut down last fall. "Like, pretend," Josie says, her voice small. The gleam in her eye pleads silently.

There's a stepladder leaning against the Quonset hut. Even from outside I can smell the chemical stench: sharp, like cat urine and rotten eggs. The ladder is short so we have to pull ourselves up, hands gripping the edge of the asphalt shingles, knees swinging sideways to crawl onto the slope. When I was sixteen it was a lot easier and when we reach the top we're both out of breath but Josie is giggling. Car lights slide by on the highway and I watch them nervously, as if expecting my mom and dad to show up. But it isn't that. Instead I'm thinking about my kids' parents, what would happen if Officer Gagnon came, whose son is in my class.

Carefully, Josie pulls two cigarettes out of her jacket. "I never came up here," she says, rolling them in her fingers so I can smell the minty aroma.

"Yes, you did," I say, although I know she's right. Usually she was in the house, her body encircled by an arm—Bruce's or, before him, another guy. Kevin, then James. I take one of the cigarettes even though I want to refuse.

"Found these in Bruce's truck," Josie says.

"Menthol?" I ask as she inhales hard, as if hungry, and lets the peak of the roof support her.

"Headrush," she says. I light mine but don't suck the smoke into my lungs, at least not at first. Then it's like something hard and adult abandons me and I lean back, loosened, and laugh. After a minute she starts telling me about the rhubarb pies she'll make, how we'll lick our plates for the last of the sweet, gummy pulp. When she stops talking there's a silence between us because I'm not sure what to say. It isn't the same, sitting up there, only the two of us. I miss Lara. I look across the field at the empty screen and suddenly Josie sits up like she's remembered something important.

"We should start it up again," she says. "Get a loan. Do it all old-fashioned with nineteen-fifties intermission movies and shit like that."

"Hmmm," I say.

"I mean it."

"I have a job," I tell her, and toss my burning cigarette over the edge.

Bruce isn't home but Josie doesn't say anything about it. I carry the box into their backyard and watch in the wash of yellow from the sensor lights as she digs a hole beside her immaculate garden. The new tomato plants a fragile green blur inside their clear plastic domes. She lowers the plant, soaks it with the hose and then pushes the earth back in. Gently, she pats down the dirt and sits back on her heels. The forest circling her yard is dark and quiet and when she stands and wipes her hands on her jeans I remember us building forts back there, eating cucumber-and-mayonnaise sandwiches under the cedars, imagining our lives. We're so still that the lights go out and Josie waves her arms to turn them on like a shipwreck survivor who's seen a boat.

Inside, we have a few glasses of wine and watch re-runs of *Buffy the Vampire Slayer*. We don't really talk. It's late so I stay over, on the blow-up mattress in the room that Josie's still hoping will be a nursery, although they've been trying for years. In the dark, I lie there wondering when it will happen and am filled with sudden longing. Only Sam has a baby, a girl Josie and I met over the Christmas holidays mostly because Sam wanted to show off. We held her at Sam's parents' place out on the lake, in the den where we used to have slumber parties. I can't sleep so I text Lara but she doesn't answer. Out, probably, at some glamorous gallery opening or late-night poetry reading, although I know that really she's probably asleep.

In the morning, I leave before Josie wakes up. I drive to both grocery stores before I find what I'm looking for: a strawberry-rhubarb pie, frozen, but it'll do. The driveway is still empty when I get back.

Josie pushes her fork into the pastry. It's tough, like cardboard, like the many boxes I'd emptied of my things the day before and collapsed. She scrapes the pink filling off the bottom slab and piles it on the plate's rim.

"I can do better," she says when the truck finally rumbles up the driveway. She reaches down and cinches the belt of her housecoat.

"I know," I tell her, remembering the raspberry-chocolate birthday cake she made for her own party the spring she turned sixteen. Outside, a vehicle door slams and I stand up. Josie prods the crust, her face tight. I squeeze her shoulder. "Call you later," I say, but she doesn't answer.

Bruce stalls when he sees me. Hands in his pockets, scraping the toe of one untied work boot over the crushed gravel. After a minute, as if we're still in high school, he says, "What'd you girls do last night?"

I think about telling him. I know Josie will. But I also know what'll happen—how cool he'll find it, how he'll be over at the house with his buddies and who knows who else, breaking in through the back door, wandering room to room, reminiscing. Beers out, then the 26ers, and then the partying like no time at all has passed.

"You should just break up with her," I blurt out, as if we aren't adults, as if they haven't been married for fourteen years. "Just let her go."

He nods once. I can tell he doesn't know how else to answer. I remember one February when Lara and I were home for reading week and Lara said something at the Iron Horse Tavern about Kafka. Bruce asked, "What's that?" We both stifled giggles while Josie stared from the shadow of Bruce's shoulder, eyes narrowed, and blasted us later for being prejudiced.

"Against stupid people?" Lara asked. Josie hasn't spoken to her since.

As I drive away, Bruce stands in the driveway, too nervous to go inside. He shrinks in my rear-view mirror until he's no larger than a figurine, one of those tiny brown animals that used to come in tea boxes, that Josie's grandmother collected. I think about the stolen plant in Josie's backyard. Those wrinkled green leaves fanning open, the rosy limbs thickening with bitter sugars. How big it will get, how soon.

Wasaga500
Megan Findlay

The others have moved the go-karts from the shed and onto the asphalt track when Marshall arrives. The boys lean against the helmet rack and watch him fishtail his grandfather's Tercel in the parking-lot. The girls at the snack bar hose bird shit off the picnic tables, their Wasaga500 T-shirts rolled up and knotted. It's the sort of day that will deliver few customers until late in the afternoon, when they'll arrive in glazed carloads from the beach, complaining about the heat and the cost of a lap around the track.

Marshall walks across the lot and pauses at the door of the shed, half in the sun and half out of it. He looks past the boys, across the track and toward the field tower under its lemon-coloured umbrella. Then he turns into the shed, where the sudden darkness half blinds him. He pats his hands along the workbench until he finds a pencil and his timecard.

Feversham, says Wiersma, watching from the shadows of his office. Marshall stops. Though they've been using it all summer, the name of his hometown still pulls hard on him. You'd better not be writing down 8 AM.

8:17, says Marshall.

He follows Wiersma into the parking-lot, where the heat floods his clothes like a bath. Wiersma punches the back of the helmet rack and the guys on the other side lurch away. The ticket girl, Wanda, leans out of the booth, fanning herself with coupons for the soft serve. She places a cigarette in the centre of Wiersma's outstretched palm. A ribbon of shade cuts across his face as he lights it.

You're staying right next door, Feversham. You can't be on time?

It's my grandfather, Marshall says. Wiersma stares out at the track until Marshall catches on and starts walking. Wiersma calls to him. When Marshall turns, a ring of keys hits him in the ribs like a bullet.

Don't look at me like that, Wiersma says. Toughen up. You're closing today. In this town we learn to be on time.

Marshall hears Wanda laugh as he fishes the keys from the grass and carries on walking. At least the boys are decent enough to look away.

It continues to surprise him, how much his grandfather has shrunk since Christmas. After his parents had dropped him off and returned to Feversham, Marshall sat on the couch next to the old man, the list of chores his mother had written still clutched in his hand. His grandfather began to cough and that's when Marshall understood what the milk pail was for. He finished spitting and looked at Marshall with his watery eyes. It's no picnic, he said. His voice rattled as if something had come loose in his throat.

Normally they'd see each other at Easter when Marshall and his parents would pack a four-course meal into a laundry basket and drive an hour to the farm, but this year his final round of mid-terms tethered him to his desk. His parents went alone and they came back with the idea that Marshall would live out there for his last summer before university. You'll be glad you did, his mother had said, which meant, I'm not giving you a choice. Why not, said his father, which meant, We can see you don't have any friends around here anyway. Marshall agreed to go because he could not think of a reason to stay home. Or rather, he could not explain the reason. But he felt it, especially in those last days of spring before he left, when he couldn't eat a meal or mow the lawn without thinking, this is the last time I'll eat dinner with my mother and father, or this is the last time I'll kick mud from those corkscrew blades. He knew this was both true and not true. He would spend the summer with his grandfather, and in the fall he would live with a boy named Alvin whose photo was stapled to his dorm-room paperwork, and then he supposed he would live in a city somewhere and never come home, not really, not in the same way. He saw his life unspooling ahead of him

124

like thread that he would have to gather slowly, day after day.

On his first night alone with his grandfather, Marshall stared hard at the list of chores in his hand, a shelf of tears rising before his eyes. He had never been in this farmhouse without his mother and father filling the cavernous rooms with conversation. Marshall shoved the thought away and tried to get himself moving. He applied lotion to the blisters that pooled below his grandfather's breastbone, then helped him onto the toilet and, an eternity later, off of it. He loved this man. He looked into the toilet bowl, freckled with muddy stains, and saw that he'd have to protect that love. He decided that he would need a way to miss his grandfather. Something to keep him at a distance for a few hours a day. It was the only alternative he could think of to a summer spent sitting on the couch, listening the sounds of his grandfather's decline.

He thought of the go-kart track first because they used to go there together, his thumb hooked in his grandfather's belt. Afterward, they'd walk home through the fields and discuss each hairpin turn. This memory abated Marshall's guilt when he went to work, leaving his grandfather alone on the couch. When he returned, the two of them would sit out on the porch, rotten everywhere but a few square feet below the kitchen window, and Marshall would read Dickens out loud. It was not an altogether terrible way to spend a summer.

Marshall is damp with sweat by the time he reaches the field tower. He seizes the ladder and climbs into the shade of the umbrella. A single customer in the batting cages hits a fly ball, and the sound falls like a drop of ice water through the hot, lifeless air.

Marshall removes a pair of binoculars from a box attached to his seat. He looks into the box then down into the grass, where he sees his book, bulging from last night's rain. Someone must have dropped it there. It's no picnic, Marshall thinks. He sits back in the guard chair and looks through the binoculars. Their only customer leaves the batting cages and walks slowly past the snack bar, waving at the girls. At first he seems headed for Wanda at the go-kart ticket counter. The boys in the pit begin to stir. But the man turns toward his car and everyone goes slack again.

125

These boys are Eric and Sam and Barry. They sometimes share a look with Marshall when they see Wiersma approaching, but that's where their friendship begins and ends. Hey Feversham, they'd say when their circuit of jokes came back around to him, the girls as skanky in your town as they are here? Marshall would attempt to look cool. Any good this ever did was undone when he was seen carrying a book to the field tower, permanently drawing a line with him on one side and everyone else on the other.

Midway through the morning two colossal RVs pull into the parking-lot. Marshall watches through the binoculars as people climb out and look around. There is one kid, a boy, who veers for the snack bar. A man's arm snaps out and yanks him back.

While the adults wait in line at the ticket window, this kid stands on his toes beside a ruler painted on the shed wall. He is too short for a solo kart. He hooks his fingers through the fence and watches Eric and Sam, who are not above showing off, even for a little kid. Five or six of the guys from the RVs pick out helmets and wedge themselves inside the karts. Wiersma swaggers over to where their women stand along the fence.

The kid climbs into the passenger seat of a double. Barry does his belt while the kid spins the dummy steering wheel. The driver of the kart guns it out of the pit, then slows a bit on the first bend. When they come level with him, Marshall shouts at them to keep their hands inside.

On their second lap, the kid and his driver pull out ahead of the pack and are nearly even with Marshall's tower when the driver cranes around, trying to see who's on his tail. These karts are meant to be slow but Wiersma disabled the governors to give the track a reputation for speed. The kart with the kid in it begins to drift. Marshall shouts and the driver corrects himself, the rest of the pack catching up and splitting around him like marbles poured from a bag.

Marshall figures he knows the type of guy driving this kid's car. The sort to have a traumatized pit bull at the end of a chain. The sort to show off at the go-kart track because younger guys have edged him from the beach. Marshall watches the throng of karts careen over the finish line a second time. Barry is waiting to take their lap ticket but the two karts out front, a single and the double carrying the kid, don't slow down. Marshall sees Barry open his mouth to shout, but no-one's paying attention.

It happens as they round the corner nearest Marshall's tower. First only a nudge from the single, then a full side push from the double. The rear wheels of the single lift clean from the pavement and into the rubber tires that line the track's inside curves. Marshall stands and turns to get down the ladder, terrified that he'll have to whisper comforts to some meathead with a broken neck. But when his feet touch ground, he sees that the kart hasn't flipped, only punched a hole in the rubber barrier and skidded out on the grass. The double has spun right around and is stalled a little ways up the track. The kid sits frozen in his seat. His helmet has slid right down over his eyes.

Asshole, shouts the kid's driver, untangling himself from the seatbelts. The guy in the single, who doesn't seem to have a seatbelt on at all, stands up.

So you're all right? calls Marshall.

Oh come on, says the other guy. Come on, man.

Listen, says Marshall. Neither man pays him any attention. Marshall glances toward the pit and sees Wiersma detach himself from the fence and take a step toward them.

Are we all okay? Marshall says. Everyone good?

The kid's driver throws down his helmet and rushes at the other guy's gut. They stagger backward, tangling themselves in the scattered tires and falling shoulders-first onto the pavement. Marshall holds up his hand to the other karts, still a turn away, but he knows it's useless. People always forget what they're doing at a time like this, lean on the gas instead of the break, turn into the accident instead of away from it, their faces blank as the sky. He tries to plant his feet near the kid, who's still sitting in the stalled double, but he already feels his muscles coiling, preparing to launch his body out of the way. From the edge of his vision he sees Wiersma break into a run, unclipping a CB radio that everyone knows is a piece of shit.

The men on the ground also notice the approaching karts. They spring apart and each plows a shoulder into the front of the stalled double. It's like seeing two extensions of a single human being. They push, their faces flushing red while the wheels under the kart scud across the pavement. The kid sways like a doll, still strapped to his seat. Kart after kart whips cleanly past them through the gap, people rubbernecking but managing to stay steady. When the last of them strips by, the two guys reel over the barrier onto their hands and knees, staring at the grass like they've lost something.

Wiersma arrives, out of breath and waving his radio. I've got the cops on the other end of this, he says.

We're cool, says the single driver, getting to his feet. He reaches down and hauls the kid's driver up.

Off the property, says Wiersma.

Marshall doesn't want hell for standing around, so he begins to work on the kid's seatbelt. When that's done he knocks on the helmet. If you're not my dad, the kid says, then I don't want to see you. He has skinny knees that stick out like knuckles. Hurry the hell up, says one of the drivers. Marshall finds the kid's small hand and helps him to his feet. He removes the helmet. The kid looks older than he'd guessed, maybe ten or eleven, though he's short, a real schoolyard shrimp with a buzz-cut and a sunburn under his eyes. What was this, asks Marshall, pointing to the remains of a temporary tattoo speckled across the kid's cheek. The Hulk, says the kid. Cool, says Marshall. Yeah, says the kid, his eyes following the karts still whipping around the track. Then he turns and walks off after the others, swinging his fists at his sides. One of the men reaches out and grips the back of the kid's neck, steering him toward the parking-lot.

Everyone is supposed to help get the karts away at the end of the day, but it's the closer who really does all of the work, refuelling the fleet and cashing out and hauling the signs in from the highway. An enormous silence falls around Marshall when he retraces his steps from that morning, back across the parking-lot to the Tercel. He sits on the hood and listens for the phantom drone of parties down at the beach. He thinks of that kid with the Hulk tattoo. Then he thinks of the hand that flashed out and gripped the kid's neck. It wasn't a gentle hand.

Marshall sits up and looks at the highway. Left is the farm. Right is Wasaga Beach and, a little way beyond that, the Whispering Pines campground, the only place he can think of where two RVs might park for the night.

The nicest thing about the Whispering Pines, as far as Marshall can tell, is a snow-white fence that rises like a wave on either side of the entrance and connects at the top in an arch. Inside the fence is a field studded with tents and trailers and camper vans. Marshall expects someone to stop him and ask him what he's doing there. A woman stands near a barbecue, swatting flies with a spatula. A man in unlaced running shoes lifts a case of beer onto one shoulder and a toddler onto the other. Ordinarily Marshall would be at the farmhouse by now, the last of the light slipping from his lap as he reads to his grandfather, his voice disappearing like smoke over the farmyard. It seems hard to believe that this world has always existed so close to that one.

He finds the RVs parked shoulder-to-shoulder at the back of the property. They look deserted until Marshall sees a woman hanging laundry on a slackening rope. He parks and looks around the car until he finds a pair of his grandfather's clip-on sunglasses. The woman hears the scuff of his shoes and turns around.

I think someone in your group left these at the go-karts today, he says. I was in the area.

Her eyes drop from his face to the glasses in his hand. No, she says. I really don't think so.

Oh, says Marshall. The RV's screen door opens and an unfamiliar boy wanders over and leans into her legs.

Hi buddy, Marshall says.

You want something? asks the woman.

He looks away. She does not mean, Do you want a drink. She means, Could you please leave.

No, he says. Sorry to bother you. I was in the area.

He drives back through the campground a little faster than when he'd come in. He can no longer remember what he'd been thinking when he arrived. He's nearly at the archway when he recognizes the boy bent over in the dirt, picking at a cigarette butt. Marshall leans out his window. Hey, he shouts, I wouldn't do that. That's dirty.

The kid attaches the butt to his bottom lip. It clings there like a dry leaf.

Marshall says, Remember me?

The kid walks over to the car. My dad almost got killed today, he says. The cigarette rises and falls as he speaks. That's what my mom told him.

My name is Marshall.

The kid stares. I'm not supposed to tell people my name, he says.

I don't need to know your name, says Marshall. I just want you to know that I'll give you a free ride on the go-karts if you ever come back.

Well anyway, it's Antonio.

That's cool. Come back sometime and I'll hook you up, Antonio.

My dad's not allowed back. The kid removes the cigarette and flicks it away.

Well, says Marshall, easing a little on the break so the car begins to roll, the karts are yours.

The kid stares.

See you, says Marshall.

At first he registers only a man shuffling along the highway's gravel shoulder toward the beach, probably a drifter. Marshall is passing the go-kart track, imagining the farmhouse and the evening rituals that wait for him there. Then he comes level with the man at the side of the road and shock drops through him like a cold stone.

I came to find you, says his grandfather, after Marshall pulls over and runs across the road. I was desperate. I couldn't make out the number you'd written down.

Here, Grandpa, take my arm.

I was desperate, his grandfather says again, and this time he parts his shirt where the buttons aren't done up.

God, Grandpa, Marshall whispers, and reaches out as if to touch the rash, which the day before had been no larger than a playing card.

I can't stand it, says his grandfather, rubbing his palms all over his chest and stomach and sides. I think it will drive me mad, Marshall.

I'm so sorry, Marshall says. He says it over and over. His hands tremble as he opens the passenger door. His grandfather is so small that it seems unlikely the seatbelt will hold him in if it needs to.

I thought you'd be home by five, says his grandfather. I thought that's what you'd said. His voice is apologetic, not accusing.

They drive through the beach town, the sunset on one side and storefronts on the other, displaying spin-racks of postcards and novelty mugs. Marshall goes as fast as he dares. The hospital is on the other side of town, facing the Wal-Mart. Marshall parks a few feet from the emergency-room doors, but it seems to take them an hour to walk that distance, his grandfather's hand gripping his own. A nurse inside takes their information and nods to the chairs in the waiting-room. Her mildness calms Marshall a little. He watches the evening news tick across a silent television screen. His grandfather does not stop moving, does not stop rubbing his chest. When he begins to cough, Marshall holds Kleenex under his mouth as a substitute for the milk pail. He tries the payphone more than once but it just rings and rings. Each time he hangs up he feels worse, picturing the sound filling his empty house in Feversham.

The doctor who sees them is used to treating old people, Marshall can tell. He winks and makes a joke about too many late-night parties while Marshall eases his grandfather's arms out of his shirtsleeves. He wishes they would turn off a few lights. His grandfather's back looks especially naked under their 1000-watt stare. Marshall thinks of all the old people in the world who find themselves on exam tables like this one, knowing that their lives will only get worse. He wants to put his arm around his grandfather's shoulders but instead he hangs back, folding and refolding the shirt in his hands. When he hears the word "shingles" for the first time, he thinks of the black tarred roof on the farmhouse.

It's dark when they leave. Marshall's grandfather holds the prescription in his fist like a winning lottery ticket. He refuses to let Marshall put his shirt back on. The doctor has rubbed his torso with cream, giving him an amphibious glow under the streetlamps. Marshall drives directly across the street to Wal-Mart, where he leaves his grandfather in the car and dashes for the pharmacy. He comes back with the pills and a bag of McDonald's for dinner.

Marshall places the bag of food on his grandfather's knees. You seem much better, he says.

It's no picnic, replies his grandfather.

I don't really have to work, Marshall says. I could stay home to help you more. I want to.

His grandfather only closes his eyes and nods. His hands lie still on either side of the bag of food. Marshall begins rehearsing the next day's conversation with Wiersma.

They drive back through the beach town and are nearly past the go-kart track when Marshall sees a silhouette lumped at the top of the security fence. It rolls off, extends into the shape of a boy, then disappears in the weeds below.

There's a kid in the go-karts, Marshall says, and stops the car. He no longer feels capable of panic. I think I know who it is, he says. Are you all right here for a minute?

I'll come, says his grandfather.

Pardon?

You said it was a kid. I'll give him this. He pokes the bag of McDonalds.

It's such an unexpected proposal that for a moment Marshall doesn't react. Then he turns and sees the boy dash across the parking-lot and around a corner of the shed. One second, he says to his grandfather, and he gets out of the car and runs across the road, fishing the keys from his pocket. He opens the gate and crosses the dark lot. At the edge of the shed he feels a moment of doubt, but he forces himself to speak.

Antonio?

There is no movement from around the corner.

This is breaking and entering, Marshall says. He tries to see around the corner without scaring the kid. Where are your parents?

I told them I'm out riding bikes.

I could call the police on you.

The boy's face flashes around the corner. He points behind Marshall. Who's that?

Marshall turns and sees his grandfather leaning into the gatepost at the edge of the parking-lot, still naked from the waist up, clutching the food bag. Marshall hesitates. Then he goes to the shed's sliding door and fits his key in the padlock. The door makes a screeching sound as he shoulders it aside. Antonio's hand darts into his.

Wait here, Marshall says, but the kid will not let go. All right, says Marshall. Come on. But Jesus, let's hurry before someone sees us.

They cross the parking-lot under the security light. The kid seems to know exactly what to do. He inserts himself under the old man's shoulder, putting his small arm around the narrow waist and leading the first step forward. Marshall's grandfather winces a little where Antonio's arm touches his bare skin, but he manages to walk. Marshall corrals the group from the other side. Inside the shed door, Marshall feels his grandfather's chest heave against him, but when he touches his hand to the old man's shoulder his grandfather only says, Who's this little fellow?

Antonio, says the boy.

Antonio does not find it strange when Marshall's grandfather thrusts the bag of food at him. He holds it at his side, like a present he's been told to open later.

I'm ten, he says.

I'm 87, says Marshall's grandfather.

Marshall waits for his eyes to adjust a little. He touches the keys in his pocket to reassure himself. It's not stealing if he has the keys.

He pulls the cord on the first double he can find, and the noise is even more monstrous than he'd feared. He's sure they can hear it all the way down at the beach. He swings himself into the driver's seat and eases the kart onto the lot, where the noise levels out a little. He gets out and looks around, but the highway is deserted.

He fits his grandfather in the passenger side, nice and easy. Antonio is skinny enough to wedge himself into the middle. Marshall finds helmets for each of them. It strikes him as a prissy thing to do, but then again, who's there to see? The boy opens his visor so he can eat French fries from the bag between his feet.

You shouldn't do things like this, Marshall shouts to the kid over the motor. Antonio nods. Okay, says Marshall. Guess we'd better go.

Aside from moving them into the shed each night, Marshall hasn't had much chance to drive the karts, and he's forgotten how low they are, how stiffly they handle. It takes him two or three turns to really get going, to feel the machine through the palms of his hands. He steals a glance at the boy and his grandfather. They each grip the dummy steering wheel, hand over hand.

He aims for the hole punched in the barrier by the accident. They leave the pavement with a fantastic lurch and swerve across the lawn, pitching over the earth as Marshall tries to hold their course. They do donuts and figure-eights and mad dashes for the fencerow that lines his grandfather's cornfields, tearing seams in the earth with each sudden turn. Marshall's grandfather and Antonio turn their wheel when Marshall turns his, leaning with him into each curve, looking with him up at the sky for the briefest of moments, sending their shouts into the air above them.

Later, Marshall will pull Antonio's BMX from the ditch weeds along the highway and fit it into the Tercel. He will drive Antonio to the Whispering Pines and pull over at a place that the little boy indicates, not too close to the front gate but not too far, and Antonio will throw one leg over the saddle of his bike and disappear under the white arch. Then Marshall will get his grandfather home and they will both sink into the couch, as if for a moment their bodies are the same old age. Eventually Marshall will leave for university, and he will begin writing weekly letters to his grandfather, then monthly letters, then only half-starts at letters that will never quite get sent. When his mother calls with the news, Marshall will rely on his roommate Alvin to sit him down under a blinking neon sign and supply him with round after round of cheap beer. Afterwards they will buy a bag of fast food and hail a cab back to their dorm, and Marshall will smell those French fries and find himself describing the night of the go-kart ride to the driver while Alvin passes out in the seat next to him. Marshall will remember the kart stalling in the middle of the grass, abandoning the three of them to abrupt silence, feeling the consoling warmth of each other's bodies. When he realizes that there is no-one to confirm the story—that his grandfather is dead, that Antonio is forever lost to the world—he adds one more detail. He says that they drove right through the cornfields, cutting a path with the front of the kart all the way from the track to the farmhouse, and that the kart stalled clean in the middle of the farmhouse lawn. And even though he's certain this didn't happen, this coda strikes him as the best story he has ever told.

Old Man Marchuk
Kevin Hardcastle

Two narrow beams of halogen light crisscrossed over the black prairie, found the warped and weathered sideboards of old man Marchuk's barn. An eerie blue round settled over the chained and padlocked barndoor handles. Up into the light rose a three-foot boltcutter. One man held the flashlight steady. One man slid the cutter-blades over the padlock shackle and squeezed hard on either handle. He had to reset twice before he'd cut through. The man with the light fussed with the lock until he freed it and could pull the chains clear. Then he pocketed the flashlight in his coveralls while he dragged the great barn doors open, his face lit like a jack-o'-lantern.

The cutter man had gotten to their one-ton pickup and he was backing it over toward the barnmouth, pushing a tow trailer by the hitch. He stopped short enough for the other man to loose and unfold the ramp to the trailer. The man in the truck waited while his partner hotwired a pair of four-wheelers and drove the first up the ramp onto the trailer bed, engine growling high. He parked it and went back for the other. Drove it into place and shut the engine off. The driver of the truck drummed the windowframe and watched, red cherry of his smoke glowing in the black. The other man raised the trailer ramp and fixed it shut. He started for the passenger side of the truck and froze three steps out.

They'd not heard the squelching of bootfalls in the thawmud near the barn. Not until the old man was right on top of them with his twelve-gauge raised high, stock pinned against his shoulder. Marchuk pulled and sprayed the driver's door. Muzzlefire showed him briefly against the outer blackness. The driver barked like a dog, ducked low and tried to cover up. Marchuk took aim again. The young man at the rear of the truck pitched his flashlight and it flew end over end past old man Marchuk's wild-haired head. Marchuk spun and fired blindly at the spot. The young man dropped to the muck and shrieked. He'd taken shot in the side and through his upper leg but he managed to clamber onto the trailer and fall in behind the last four-wheeler just as his buddy punched the gas and sent the truck tires spinning. The old man had shucked his spent shells and set about reloading the firearm. Marchuk emptied both barrels on the truck and its trailer as the vehicle sped off serpentine through his fenceless backfields.

He came upon the trailered vehicle not ten miles down the county road. The driver sped just slightly and held the road straight. Marchuk drove an old Dodge pickup and he had his running lights turned off. He drifted up alongside the larger truck until he could see both men sitting stung in the cab. When the driver turned and saw the old man coasting along beside him he panicked and swerved wide, caught the edge of the roadside drainage ditch and pulled back. The trailer nearly jackknifed before skittering back in line on the weatherbuckled asphalt. Old man Marchuk cut into the other lane and the driver of the one-ton chickened out and slammed his brakes, went too far wide this time and ended up ploughing sanded ditchturf for about a hundred feet before the vehicle shuddered to a stop. Marchuk got out with the scattergun and pumped holes through the driver door.

Constable Tom Hoye got the call from dispatch and had to floor it from two townships over. He saw four red eyes in the road and then felt a series of little thuds on the car's undercarriage. He drove on. The constable had lately been stationed at the lonely RCMP detachment that served the county, with its three-man rotation and one dispatch to cover four barren townships. They got calls of gunfire a few times a week and heard gunfire every night. That night was the first they'd gotten a call from the man who actually fired the shots, and that man went by the name of Marchuk. Hoye took the details as he drove.

"What's he sayin' he shot at?" Hoye said.

"Two men tryin' to steal his ATVs," said the girl at dispatch. "But he's not sayin' he shot at them. He's sayin' he shot them."

"What?"

"How far out are you?"

"Seven or eight minutes. Where's the EMT?"

"They won't be a minute behind you if at all."

When Constable Hoye pulled up to the scene he saw the one-ton tipped over in the ditch, shrapnel and shards of windowglass that shone by the light of the cruiser's headlamps. Marchuk was leaning up against the side of his own truck, one foot crossed over the other, cradling his shotgun in the crook of his arm. The old man put one hand up against the headlights. Constable Hoye got out of the car with his hand on his pistol. He flicked the safety off as he stood. Marchuk just waited there, taking the air as the constable came over. Plains wind travelled warm and gentle through the pass. The faint sound of ambulance sirens called out from afar.

"Set your firearm down on the ground and step away," Hoye said.

Marchuk frowned at him. Hoye had to pull his pistol and let it hang before the old man knelt and laid the weapon down on the tarmac. The constable waited until Marchuk stepped clear and then he gestured for him to keep going.

"Put your hands on the hood of your truck," he said.

"Son, you are wastin' my time," the old man said.

"Put your fuckin' hands on the hood I said. And stay put."

Marchuk sauntered over and did it, slapping his palms down like a showy child. He stood there in his coveralls. Sandpaper beard and huge, crooked nose. Hoye passed him and stepped down into the ditch. Took his flashlight out of his belt and turned it on. When he shone the beam over the ditchhill he saw pieces of the truck's upholstery scattered across the turf like cottongrass, a full section of door siding with thin furrows in the mould. Then he saw the two shot men. One was on his side in the ditchbasin, his legs shuffling. The other lay starfished against the hillside in his bandit-blacks and he didn't move at all.

"Jesus fuckin' Christ," Hoye said.

He started to go for the men and then he stopped and levelled his pistol at Marchuk. The old man took his hands off the hood and put them up until Hoye barked at him to put them back. The constable came back into the road and took out his cuffs and braceletted the old man's bony wrists.

"Just what the fuck are ye doin', son?" said Marchuk.

"You shot those men?"

"They were robbin' me."

"Your farm is fuckin' three miles thataway," Hoye said, nodding south.

The old man stared at him sourfaced. The back of his scraggly head lit up in colours. An EMT wagon crested a rise in the roadway and coasted toward them. Hoye stepped out into the lane and waved it down.

He came home an hour before sunrise, the sky paling to the east. The constable and his wife had rented a two-story brownstone with no house number. Just their name stencilled on the mailbox. Their nearest neighbour was a gravel quarry some three miles away. Hoye parked the cruiser on the driveway and went into the house through the sideporch entrance. He hung his keys and undressed, put his jacket and his Kevlar over the back of a wooden dining-table chair. Laid his pants overtop, flat to the crease. Then he went to the fridge and knuckled up two bottles of beer. He sat on the living-room couch with the TV on but nearly inaudible. The bottles were empty after maybe five pulls so he got up to grab another.

Hoye's eyes had turned to slits when the stairwell groaned behind him. He stood up and saw his wife descending slowly, tiny bubble of tongue bit between her lips as she concentrated on landing each footfall. She followed a dogleg near the stairbottom and made her way down the last three steps. The young woman stood maybe five-foot-three with copper hair and a round, round belly pushing up the cloth of her nightie.

"Hey," she said. "Nice outfit."

Hoye stood there in his gitch, his blues unbuttoned and his undershirt showing. He had the legs of a quarterhorse.

"What time is it, Jenny?" he said.

"It's not morning and it's not night," she said.

He watched her shuffle past the couch and she eyed him sidelong as she went. She started smiling, deep dimple at her right cheek.

"If you sneezed I think you might pop," he said.

"Are you gonna go to bed or what?" she said.

"I didn't really think that far ahead."

"What happened out there?"

"That old fella Marchuk pumped about six rounds of buckshot into two city boys who were stealin' his ATVs."

"My God," she said. "Are they alive?"

He nodded.

"Somehow."

"How was he when you took him?"

"He didn't think he did nothin' wrong."

She went into the kitchen and he heard the cupboards opening and closing. He came in to help her but she shooed him. Hoye got behind his wife and put his arms around her shoulders, held the belly in his big hands, his chin pinned to her shoulderblade. She reached up and cupped his cheek.

"Get off me you big oaf," she said, but she didn't move. Finally he kissed her neck and stood up tall, let her loose.

"Go to bed for a couple hours," Jenny said. "I'm not going anywhere."

So he did.

The two young burglars didn't die but came about as close to it as they could. The driver lost one of his feet and the meat of his right triceps and he had nerve damage throughout. The other burglar flatlined three times during surgery and that was after he'd almost bled out in the ambulance. They were under police guard and would be until they were fit for trial. But not their trial. They had pled guilty by proxy and were sentenced to community service and probation. The trial they awaited was Marchuk's. The old man had been arraigned and pled not guilty before cussing out the court and the sitting judge.

The old man had lands and money enough to post his bail-bond, high as it was, but some folks from that township and those that bordered somehow anted up the cost and posted for him. On a pretty autumn day Marchuk left the stationhouse shaking his head and then he drove back to his farm in his old

Dodge. There he took back the tending of his property from cousins who had driven in from north-interior British Columbia. They didn't go back. Instead they shacked up with him and awaited the trial.

The first attack against Hoye was no more than the rude spray painting of the words "Eastern Pig" on his garage door. He managed to acetone the graffiti clear before his wife got a chance to see it. Hoye heard rumblings of who might have done it and he let it be known that the drinking age in that county was about to be enforced nightly. Fines to be given out and liquor to be confiscated. Two weeks later somebody tore up the sideyard of his house by spinning doughnuts all over the crabgrassed turf. It happened when he was out on patrol and when he got home he found Jenny on the porch steps with a pump shotgun on her lap. Shells in a line on the wooden planking beside her. He had to talk a long time before he could get his gun back. They went inside and sat together in the kitchen.

"What, are they retarded or something?" she said.

"They just ain't accustomed to having someone tell them no. But they're gonna figure it out real quick."

Jenny sipped at a glass of water, the fingers of her right hand lightly stained with gungrease.

"He nearly killed those kids."

"They think it was justified."

"We don't live in Texas."

"If we did he'd still be locked up. They would've had to be inside his house for him to open fire."

"How much longer do we have before you can pick a new station?"

"One year, three months, and eighteen days."

Jenny stood up slowly. Took up his empty beer bottle and carried it over to the counter. She got him another from the fridge and set it down.

"I just hope they quit it."

Hoye pulled hard on the bottle, set it down on the kitchen table and stared at it. At the rough hand holding it.

"They will," he said.

Jenny Hoye drove over an hour to get to the nearest big-box store. She took trips there weekly to load up on diapers and formula, toiletries, other household necessaries. From those narrow, sunbaked roads she saw miles and miles of shortgrassed dunes, low-rolling plains with not a pond or trickle of river. Rare sightings of stunted trees with their barks dried and sloughing. Remains of groundhogs and coyotes on the macadam or otherwise strewn in the roadside gravel. Once in a while a lonely oilfield pumpjack with its counterweight turning anticlockwise and its steel horsehead dipping low and rising again. There was a base and barracks in the town and on her visits she would see men in army camos trailing their wives down the aisles, some upright and solemn and others leaning down heavy to the carthandles as they shoved along.

She filled her cart and pushed it to the checkout line. When she rung through a young stockboy with a hairlip asked her if she needed a hand getting out. Jenny told him thanks but she'd be okay. He smiled shyly and went on. She wheeled the cart out into the lot and found her parking spot. As she was loading the trunk she heard someone calling her name. Jenny turned to see a young woman hailing her from across the lot.

"Fuck," she said.

On the way home she saw a four-door pickup in her rearview mirror and it stayed there. Monster tires and a heavy steel grillguard. Mud and muck on the hood and windshield. Jenny drove through town and took a turn that she didn't need to take and the truck kept on straight. She snaked home through the county roads and there on the last length of dirt lane the jacked-up truck stood idling at an intersection, not a half-mile from her house. It pulled into the lane behind her and followed close. She could see sunburned forearms hanging thick on either side of the vehicle. There were at least four men, two in front and the rest in back. She nearly drove on past the house but cut a hard right at the last second and skittered onto the gravel driveway. The truck slowed but kept on. Four sets of eyes on the woman as she got out and studied the vehicle and the muddied British Columbia plates. A gun rack had been fixed in the back window of the truck and all the brackets were full.

Hoye pulled into the farm's frontlot at dusk with two cruisers trailing him. He saw lamplight through the thin-curtained upper windows. Brighter lights in the kitchen. The sound of country music and raised voices travelling raucous from an open side door. There was no proper driveway, just a ruined patch of land in front of the house filled with vehicles. Battered pickups and rusted out car frames on blocks and a gargantuan RV parked sidelong to the house, power cables running between the two like tentacles. A raised, extended-cab pickup with B.C. plates. Hoye pulled in first and the other cars followed. Each cruiser rode two officers and they got out armed and armoured and Hoye took two of them toward that kitchen side-entry. Hoye was certain that there would be dogs to give them away early, but there were not.

When they walked in through the kitchen screendoor it squealed on its springs. Four men sat at a massive oak-slab table with bottles of beer and whiskey staining the lumber. Two women were tending the stove. One middle-aged and greying, stout and squarejawed. The other young and dirty blond and very pretty, a scattering of old pox-scars on her cheek and forehead. Hoye and his two constables came into the room and spread out, eyeballed the foreign men, hands on the heels of their pistols. A door shut somewhere in the back of the house and soon enough the three other constables filled the doorway at the other side of the kitchen. Hoye knocked a stack of papers from a nearby chair where it sat below a wall-mounted rotary phone. He spun the chair to the table and sat. Across from him sat old man Marchuk and he tried to stare a hole through Hoye. Black, biblical hate in his eyes. Hoye just stared back.

"You know that there's warrants out for your cousins here, from B.C., and they're to be escorted to the border and placed in custody there."

"That is a load of horseshit," Marchuk said. "What for?"

"I've got 'Fight Causing a Disturbance' for a Bretton Marchuk and 'Cultivation of Marijuana' for Gary Myshaniuk and Mark Oulette. The rest can just go in for assisting wanted fugitives."

"They're my guests and they aren't goin' anywheres. So you can go fuck yourself. You ain't got no warrant or cause to come into my house."

"We don't need a warrant to seize the wanted men. But I'll be kind and give them a chance to drive their asses outta here to the border under escort. Or they could get shot instead in this fuckin' kitchen for all I care. Seems to be a way of life for you folks."

Marchuk tried to get out of his chair and Hoye stood and sat him back down by the shoulder.

Old man Marchuk was taken into custody and locked up in the station holding cell while his cousins were driven west, handed off from detachment to detachment until they were released to officers from Golden. Bretton Marchuk had a broken nose plugged with bloody tissue when he was put under arrest inside British Columbia. The other men were marked with facial lacerations and contusions along their forearm and shinbones. The elder woman, wife to the cousin Marchuk, spat at one of the B.C. constables and then watched her husband take a baton to both of his knees. She held her spit from then on. The constables released the younger, blond woman alone, and let her take the truck back to their lands in the foothills.

Marchuk saw his bail rescinded and spent his days and nights in holding at the Red Deer Remand Centre. He got letters and visits from townsfolk. Few people would speak to Hoye or his wife, any of the other officers or their families, even those born in that township. Hoye did not mind. One day he found their lawn staked with dozens of "For Sale" signs. He pulled them and stacked them in the garage.

On shift near Daysland, Constable Hoye had his radio flare up and the dispatch told him that his wife had been taken by ambulance to the hospital in Red Deer. Jenny Hoye had gone into labour nearly a full month early. The constable lit his sirens and drove those black nightroads with the gas pedal pinned. He pulled into the hospital lot just before midnight and found triage, took directions to the labour and delivery-rooms.

Hoye wore scrubs over his uniform and they let him into delivery. Jenny gripped his hand hard. Her hair had gone dark with sweat and stuck to her forehead. She had taken no epidural and had just begun to crown. Hoye bent to better see her face.

He wiped her brow with a wet cloth and tried to get the hair from her eyes.

"It's alright, Jenny," he said.

"Oh, fuck this," she said.

The doctors had her breathe and push. She hollered and swore and gritted her teeth. Again and again until the baby's shoulders cleared. The boy was born blue with the umbilical wound tight around his neck and upper arm. The doctors went to work unwinding the cord. Jenny had gone pale and stared at the little shut eyelids and the soft skin of his discoloured arms. Blood and mucous on her gown and at her inner thighs. Constable Hoye could barely stand and he waited cold by the hospital bed. It took four minutes for the baby to breathe and when he did he spoke in a wail and reached out with his tiny arms, cycled his feet in the air.

The constable watched his wife and son through the night and spoke to the attending doctors. The boy had no ill effects from the tangled cord and he'd been born heavy for a premature baby, had a strong heart and lungs to cry with. Hoye left in the morning and he hadn't slept at all. He went to the house with a list and gathered things for his wife. He stood over the patch of kitchen floor where Jenny had been when her water broke. He didn't know whether to clean it or not. After passing it by a few times on his rounds Hoye filled a bucket with soapy water and bleach and started mopping the tile.

Jenny stayed with the baby in the maternal and newborn unit of the hospital for the better part of two weeks. Constable Hoye came every day between shifts or he had another constable cover while he left his watch for an hour or two. He spoke to his son in whispers while Jenny slept.

The Marchuk trial had been set for a neutral, closed court in Calgary. It started on a Tuesday morning and did not look like it would last a week, so shoddy was the defence. Hoye gave testimony on the third day of the trial and when he came home he found his mailbox rent apart, pebbles of buckshot rattling around inside the deformed container when he pried it clear from the post. He flung it into the garage and drove to the hardware store in town.

The clerk limped slightly as he took Hoye down the shelf rows. A tall man of nearly 70 with a white moustache and short-cropped hair. He had no glasses but seemed to need some more than a little. He showed Hoye toward the mailboxes, most of them antiquated and covered in light dust. Hoye picked out the plainest one and followed the old man toward the buckets of screws and fasteners.

"Heard you had a boy," the man said.

"We did."

The clerk offered his hand. Hoye took it. Hoye was of the same height and wider by a foot but the old man's hand outsized his by far.

"You gonna raise him here?"

"Likely not," Hoye said.

The clerk smiled a little and stood with his knuckles to his hips, picked a stray bolt from a bin and put it back where it belonged. They started back toward the register. Hoye held up.

"Hang on a minute," he said.

Hoye went back to where he'd been shown the mailboxes and he came back to the counter with a second. The clerk had set the first on the woodtop beside the till. Hoye handed him the other and the man nodded and started to tally it all. He found a cardboard box behind the counter and filled it with the goods. Hoye paid him in cash.

"I suppose I don't have to tell you to be careful out there," the clerk said.

"No. But I appreciate it."

"It's not the whole town that's sided against you, young man, or even the half of it. But those that have are awful loud. If you know what I mean."

Hoye nodded and shook the clerk's hand again.

"If you run through those two just come back and I'll get you another, on the house."

Hoye laughed. Waved at the clerk as he went out the door. Windchimes jangled where they hung from the lintel.

On a dry and sunbleached afternoon Constable Hoye pulled up to his homestead with his wife and newborn son. He'd been

146

given a week's worth of leave. A cruiser waited at the roadside near the house. Hoye stopped to say hello and the constable in the other cruiser made faces at the baby in the backseat, the little boy in a safety chair beside his mother. The other constable shook Hoye's hand.

"How're you all handling it?" Hoye said.

"They got a fella from up near Viking that makes his rounds a little further south. He don't seem to mind. Shifts go long they're givin' us OT."

"Well, thank 'em for me will ya."

"Sure," the constable said. "Keep your radio nearby. Anything comes up I'll squawk at ya."

Hoye nodded and drove on, turned onto the width of gravel in front of the house. The cruiser crept out and took off down the county road. Hoye parked and came around the car to help Jenny. He wore her many bags and bundles on his arms like he were a clothes maiden. Jenny took the boy up in her arms and swaddled him to her chest and neck. She turned him slow so that he could stare out goggle-eyed at the fields and fencewires and hovering birds.

"We get a new mailbox?" she said.

Hoye stood there with the bags dangling. He nodded.

"Old one sort of blew in. So I got another, pegged it down a little sturdier."

Jenny studied the box some more and then she kissed the baby on his pale and peachfuzzed head and went down the walk to the house. Hoye kicked the car door shut with the toe of his shoe.

Hoye lay in the bed until they both slept. When he got up he went quiet as he could, clicking sound in his knees and his left ankle joint. He turned at the door and saw the dent in the mattress where he rested his bones of a night, his tiny son but inches from it, curled up and pinned to his wife. It hurt his heart just to look at her there, wild haired as she was in sleep, snoring lightly, so much bigger than their boy. It flooded hollows in him. Cold travelled along his spine and shortribs. He didn't want to leave but he did. He'd found cargo shorts in the laundry hamper and put them on, along with a clean undershirt. He went through the dark house and he knew it less by touch than he should have.

Out on the driveway he sat, garage door open to a tiny nightlight and a fridge of cold beer. Crickets had gotten into the garage and they trilled from their hiding spots. He had an old poker table set up with cans of beer in every cup holder, a bottle of Irish whiskey standing quarter-empty on the felt. The Remington pump lay on a wooden crate beside his chair, five cartridges in the magazine. Chinook wind blew warm across the prairie, slowly spun a crooked weathervane that had been long ago fixed atop the high front gable of the house. Hoye had his Kevlar on over his cottons and the shirtcloth clung to his stomach and lower back. He heard distant reports of riflefire. High whine of small engines. Coyotes whooping at each other in a nearby field. Hoye sat there and watched either end of the long, country road. His portable CB radio sat on the table, silent except for sparse chatter between the dispatch and the constables as they roamed the territories.

The Historian
Leon Rooke

Karl often, after his discovery, expected people he knew to come up to him and say something like "How is Lasalle? How is that girl?" Something like that.

Or they would say, "You're a lucky so-and-so to have a woman in your life like that firecracker Lasalle. Why could I not have been that lucky?"

They would look at him with those slant eyes, while making deep-throated noises that anyone, not just Karl, would have found disturbing.

Today he was in the Snack Parlour looking around for something interesting to look at or eat. Lots of yogurts in the fridge, a good many plastic bags containing one item or another. The owners' names written on the bags, as well as on many of the yogurt lids. Myrtle, Asiaga, Mary, Yolinda, and so forth, but no Lasalle. Not yet. Which meant that Lasalle wasn't sick like these others or if she was then she was sick in another place. Not here. Wonder why not. What was she up to, that Lasalle?

A strange woman was poking his arm. Poke, poke.

No, not strange, not strange at all, now that he gave her face some thought.

Ruth, the nurse.

Ruth was speaking. She was saying, "We have told you and told you to stay out of those yogurts. Buy your own yogurts. You're not the frenzied yogurt lover you make yourself out to be."

"I love those yogurt drinks although those up here cost triple those down there"—he was thinking Mexico—"and are not nearly as good."'

149

"You mean in hell? What I'd like to know is when they dropped the h. Yog-hurt. I much preferred the word with an h. But now everything is like that. We're like a nation of zombies, desperately influenced by *Night of the Living Dead.* On the other hand, happily adjusted people are not among my favourites. Even rodents may be happily adjusted."

Karl laughed. Ruth was a guaranteed nursing fanatic. He liked her trim eyebrows and lustrous cheeks, which so well dressed up her generally trim frame. Generally trim, though not totally. Well, who in his right mind would want a totally trim woman in the first place? You could thread a needle with...fit in a key hole....

"Sorry, Ruth," Karl said. "You were saying?"

"Your daughter is here to see you."

"Who?"

"Don't play dumb with me. She's in the lounge. We've been looking all over for you."

"I'd better spruce up a bit," Karl said. "We can't be upsetting our visitors on a night like this."

"It's two in the afternoon, Karl. Try not leaping off the pier."

No-one was in the lounge. The big TV was going and a bevy of new flowers, already shedding their blossoms, adorned the long window sill. The window, which had a vista of practically nothing, was lit with fingerprints and loopy swirls. Someone had dribbled wet patches and a bit of scum on each of the three carpets. "Those TVS have only a certain number of hours to live," Karl said, addressing the room. "About 4000, or so I have been informed. Then, like us, they go kaput."

He turned off the instrument and sat down contentedly in a red chair to watch it.

He awakened to find a wan, not quite wrinkled face staring into his own.

"You were making animal noises in your sleep," that person said. "I bet you $50 I can tell you exactly what you were dreaming."

Karl said, "What I bet is that you are not on my visitors' list. This is a classy operation. They don't allow just anyone over the threshold, you know."

The person smiled. She looked, for a moment, radiantly happy. "I love you, Daddy," she said. "You have ever been an instant joy to my eyes. You do not have any nice little contraband bottle secreted about your body, do you? Say yes, please! Are you aware that the identical cool medicinal aroma occupies every niche of this abode? It wafts through the vents, making street passersby wonderfully loopy. One acquires an immediate fix. I strolled endless corridors seeking you. The basement, I discovered, is in actuality an ancient, now long abandoned, subway stop. The line connects to countless other buildings. I walked the tracks. Morbid, I tell you! But what a complex! They are all hospitals. All are humming. I counted eight. All sharing the identical aroma, as if sprayed daily by a fleet of helicopters. I peered into each of them. Barely any disarray perceived. *Impeccable*! Excusing, of course, extended nightmare in the emergency parlours. Saving lives: the last *art*! Are you delighted to see me?"

"Why exactly are you here?"

She tousled his hair, aligned his garment neatly, submitted him to prolonged scrutiny, and a short while later seemed to be gone.

"Did you enjoy your game?" Now it was nurse Ruth—provoking?—appraising him.

The visitor—it had been his daughter, Gayle, the youngest and dearest; he wasn't entirely flummoxed by a day's events. Let's put it this way: apparitions came and went. Gaylie—she had wanted to be called Zulu, as a child—had brought along a chess set in an ornate onyx box—"Guatemalan," he told Ruth—the pieces so small they could hardly fit into the hand.

"I beat her soundly," he said. "Mercilessly. I always do. Zulu lacks focus. She doesn't apply herself. Sometimes I see in her face the glassy eyes of those dolls she played with as a child. All my daughters possess that trait."

"Me too, after a long shift. She's like a ghost around here. The other day I found her in our linen-room, sniffing the sheets. She settles rose petals on empty beds. She's nice, though a nuisance. She looks like you."

"I hope not. She's a helpless sojourner through unkempt fields, who ought to put on a few pounds."

"You noticed that? She can have mine."

"Go easy on yourself. I'm sure you have your pulchritudinous moments. Last night, about midnight, my telephone rang. It was the Police Auxiliary. The caller asked for a donation to help send young hoodlums to summer camp. Those were his exact words."

"Oh. Those calls. It could be the CIA, the Gnat Security Agency, one of those watchdogs, out to keep terrorists busy responding to trifles."

"Good grief!"

"You likely don't know this. That wayfaring daughter often overnights in your room. She sings you songs in a voice so faint and sweet we all weep. *Little Girl Blue. My Funny Valentine.*"

"Our favourites."

Karl ventured into the wrong room. It seemed to be filled to capacity with three obese girls who were of an age still to be considered children. "Someone, naming no names, has been foraging on my cupcakes," one of the girls said. The others showed a lot of teeth, laughing. Often these girls were seen as a group hurling themselves up and down the corridors and riding the elevators. Banging on doors. They seemed not to know they were obese or if they did this was something fated by life's prickly cauldron, to be worried about another day. Some while ago Karl had asked them their names. Zippo, the first said. Zappo, said the next. "Satchmo," cried the third. Then they laughed hysterically. "Got a fag? Smoking keeps oomph off the bones," continued the first. "After a fag we always like smooching a faggot."

The chief obesity had said to Karl, "Zappo and Satchmo are structurally challenged. They are tormented by indecision, like that Hamlet poof. A heavy hand is obliged. A grizzly ramrod, lest they disappear within themselves like melting chocolate. I am the ramrod of this outfit. We are home on the range, rustling everyone's cattle. Sheep-keepers, beware." She compelled him to examine the peculiar watch adorning a bulky left wrist. The watch had a colossally long tarnished silver band that wrapped like a snake up past the elbow. "It's a cobra watch," she said. "A cobra on a mission like those monks who throw themselves out of windows. Defenestrate, that's the word. You'll see on the watch-face tomorrow's date. This outfit prefers to live entirely in the future. Everyone should, in my opinion."

The two other girls practically wept with joy at these pronouncements. They stomped their feet and jiggled their hips
and the room appeared to tilt one way and another. They cried
out in unison, one going high, the other low—the Raelettes, the
Blossoms, the Cookies came to Karl's mind:

we are ice-cold bitches
when we cry
ice cubes
cascade from our eyes
we are a weeping Gibraltar
the melting north.
your hereafter.

"So you're the famous historian," the ramrod said. "What
period or realm or zone of being, life's hectic traffic, do you or
did you in your prime historicize?"

At this mention of his profession an immense variety of cloud-
less memories zipped into and out of the many rooms and closets
and antechambers of Karl's mind, like a thousand little mice
desperately seeking shelter.

The ramrod smirked. Her feet were too large for her canvas
shoes, Karl noticed. Those shoes, of Dollar Store design, were
overburdened; they'd go to their death inside the week. A sky-
blue colour, matching perfectly her beautiful eyes. "What, professor," she was asking, "is the oldest fossil ever unearthed, since
you're so hotass smart?"

These girls, obese nymphets, were a quixotic crew, Karl supposed. Even so, he would recommend a suicide watch with armed
guards ever vigilant. He had convinced himself this was that
kind of place. "Your views are utterly nonsensible," someone had
told him. "Maybe so," he recalled replying, "but it is surely a
sordid fact that one has to walk an honest mile from this place,
through ruin and dilapidation, a festering city, in order to secure
an alcoholic beverage."

"See me," a voice had whispered, but Karl, distressed, could
not determine the origin.

The obese force kindly moved on to other prey.

"All you old goats in this place are illegal homesteaders. We
mean to butcher your cattle, set ablaze your wagons, drive you

153

out. We are obese renegade Indians intent on mayhem."

"We want pizza, we want pasta, we want heaping pie-a-la-mode," sang another.

Oldest *complete* fossil *Rugosodon eurasiaticus*, if you placed your truck on Zhe-Xi Luo. Karl hadn't remembered. He had stolen his way onto a chained computer on a vacated desk in the lower lobby. He had googled. Afterwards, a tickled security man nudged him back upstairs. Before that, they had stood a good many minutes together in a doorway watching a parade of attractive women pass up and down the avenue.

Could the lost Lasalle be among them?

"In you go, professor. I were you, I'd forget that Lasalle."

"Chip—that's your name?—forgetting has become my problem."

Karl's deceased wife Louisa had liked saying to guests, "I do not always rise to my husband's expectation. I wither. He likes a saintly woman. The grandiose! Isn't that a remarkable characteristic?"

Oohs and ahhs often held sway those rare moments when Louisa elected to speak. Then a chorus would ring out *Now for another martini!*

"It's like she's the hidden queen," Karl said.

"Who? This Lasalle?"

Karl was attempting to explain to three research pioneers—mere assistants—his Lasalle dilemma. They were in a panelled room behind closed doors. The trio had the look of people who had in their time experienced a good deal of grief. Their eyes were those of caged birds, beady and wary, their heads often tilted, causing Karl to think of Moby and Prelude, two of Zulu's pet parrots during her addled bird period. Eyes closed, he could see those parrots perched on Zulu's petite fingers, calling for watermelon. Smart birds constrained by tangled memory, always falling asleep precisely at 7 PM, 6 in winter.

"Louisa and I were forever having to douse iodine over those fingers."

"Sir? What? Pardon?"

Karl said, "It is, as you likely are aware, both treasure and burden to be equipped with potent memory. The condition neither foreshadows tranquillity nor directly repulses it." Though they nodded it seemed to Karl they hardly recalled why they were here.

"Say you have before you a tuning fork that remembers not the tunes yet remains to all eyes the genuine article."

The three marvelled. Hm, they said. I think you have lost us.

Karl likewise was lost. Tuning fork? Where had he been going? But by similar means had he formulated his best lectures, drafted his best papers, written his most enduring books.

The one with the cropped hair and wide mouth stood. He said he believed it had been forced upon him the necessity to amend his previous position, namely his analysis of...his analysis of....

All waited. They waited through and past that moment when silence became an active, combative presence. Karl imagined waiting in cold night for heat from a disconnected furnace. To his knowledge this man had never offered an *analysis* of anything. This man harboured ludicrous bias against a certain obese gang. *Such commotion!* He expressed opposition to all "juvenile twaddle." Never would applaud the Raelettes. *Tomb* music would be his preference.

But be kind, Karl told himself. The engine of uniformity need not be invoked. The wrath of The Izarn need not apply; the laws of Hammurabi do not obtain. No need to rain down upon him my own bucket of abuse.

One of the woman was up fanning the man's face with a nest of blue folders. "I think Robert has fallen asleep," she said. "He's always so intense."

A serenade of soft chuckles arose. Robert was the least intense man alive. His wife had left him. Parents refused him. What idiot had hired him? Soon he would be mistaken for dead.

The obese children could be heard running along the corridor. They were screeching, "I want my cupcake!" They were young and otherwise without purpose. Karl had never seen any cupcakes in the Snack Room. He'd seen cupcake remains in the lounge, some on chipped plates and others thrown against the long vista-deprived window and in various beds belonging to whimpering adults. The girls, en masse, reminded Karl of those Henry Moore sculptures, shorn of beauty. He was about to give voice to this observation but then thought better of it. Some thoughts ought not to be put into words, although this one already had.

Snickers were heard outside the door. A note slowly surfaced on the floor.

PRE-PUBESCENT RALLY TONIGHT 8 PM IN B WING, TINKERBELL PRESIDING.

"Here's the thing about Lasalle," Karl said. "A while ago, clearing junk from the house, I came across this ratty old college yearbook. I thought I'd long ago thrown that business away. But there it was, the pages pretty much glued together. Gritty with age. Each page riddled with good will messages from hallowed classmates. Every one making reference to Lasalle. What a great girl she was. How lucky I was to have such a smart, stunning Aphrodite in my life. On and on they went in this fashion. Including in the end, in my own hand, under the heading RESERVED FOR DIVINE LASALLE, a lengthy epistle, love letter, from this very party. 'You have changed my life. I can't live without you. Your snapshot has been mangled by my kisses. You'd think a dog had got at it. Love. Love, Love, kisses many fold. I think of you and my heart thunders like horses running a derby. Yours forever and ever, Oh, my sunshine and life, my very breath!' Like that. On and on. In heart-breaking extraordinarily beautiful script. Cozy, elegant, refined. Wonderful grammar. Excellent paragraphing. Nothing misspelled. Not a dangling participle to be found. But no photograph, no student named Lasalle anywhere in the book."

"A town girl?" suggested the security guard, that pleasant fellow, Chip, custodian of the civic pulse. "I usually, usually, customarily, preferred a town girl's outpost as my larder against the lonely weekend."

"Larder?" asked Karl.

The woman at the information desk spoke up. She was not happy. "I don't see the gravity here. We all have secret gaps in our lives. Some of us have bottomless sinkholes, black pits extending past the horned remoteness of China. Your desuetude on this subject is a waste of our precious limited bodily resources. Better you employed those resources going carbon, confronting climate change, expurgating the bible and the Koran...."

"The Kama Sutra?' offered Chip.

"...Attempt something important," continued the desk woman, rifling a hand through raspberry hair. "Something rarified, principled, judicious, and ennobling. Why should I care about a vain man's stupid Lasalle, however celebrated he be?" She laughed to show she was kidding. Partly laughed. Her mirth wasn't of abiding issue. "I tell you sometimes I feel like ripping out my hair. Society has plummeted. Not only patients. The public is worse. This mores biz they tell me you write about, I could tell you a thing about that. Pants down to their knees, I can see their cracks! They stride right in demanding cigarettes! They vomit in our doorways, drink from the sanitizer bottles meant solely for hands. Well, goodness gracious, where do I stop? Your gap, Dr. Karl, painful though it be, is less grievous than many. I'm tempted to call it hackneyed rubbish. If real people can disappear, as they do every day, especially young boys and girls, why be surprised that someone who likely existed only in your mind should pull a vanishing act? That she's now a tiny figment stuck up there in your head should make you happy. I'd love to have a guy figment trapped in my brain. I'd work the little bastard night and day."

"A good memory isn't all it's cracked up to be," said Chip. "I'd be happy to have lived another's childhood. Uh-oh. Here comes the Cheese-Whiz brigade."

"Those fat girls are beyond hope," said the information specialist, kicking the desk chair until it went flying. They watched the chair strike a far wall, spring back as if in surprise, then careen in dizzying circles before it flopped over like something dead.

"I've always hated that chair," the woman said. "Almost as much as I dislike those fatties."

"They display admirable verve," Karl said. "Panache. Fortitude."

"What gruel! It is all pretence. Their sight sickens me. They bounce along like over-inflated balloons. They pose on street corners in obscene buttock skirts, showing red panties, pantaloons,

157

waving syringes I know for a fact to be fake. They juggle their bazooms like lascivious whores. Yesterday the ringleader told me she'd seen Jesus on a Starbucks couch cutting his toenails. Blasphemous idiot! She said sandals only came into existence because of the long toenails people had back then. She claimed the Romans held that long toenails were equated with success, which corresponds with the false nails and lashes women don today. How ludicrous. Those girls are so perverse, cavort so gaily, you'd think they think tomorrow they will be throwing confetti at newlyweds. Stop shaking your heads. I'm aware I sometimes make no sense."

"Illusion can be dandy," Karl said.

"I don't wish to personally engage these issues," said Chip. He paused, sighing. "However, I suppose our friend here is right in thinking it's all a ruse. "Clever, though. Antics obscure, perhaps replace, the pain. Nothing wrong with a good masquerade. They were arrested, you know. Police thought they were drunk. Drugged. A public hazard. Turned out they were clean. No booze, no drugs, nothing. They don't come near fatty foods. Actually, they've shed a bucket load of pounds. Isn't that so, professor?"

Karl, trying to compose himself—a banana Popsicle might help—thought he might finally be beginning to understand Arendt's "banal" shtick.

Karl's sleep was not without interruption. In the dream a great winged bird announced he had a visitor waiting by his bed. "But I am in my bed," Karl said. The visitor turned out to be his father spun anew from ashes, and unrecognizable. His father, dead, had more to say than when alive. "They don't let us have beds where I am," he confessed in a stately, becalmed voice not his own. "They heave us all into enormous piles, in some kind of flood plain. You spend the whole of your death attempting to scramble free. Just when you think you've made it along comes the flood to sweep you back again. It's like that Sisyphus story, the Camus version, I believe, that terrified you as a kid, imparting a notion of the futility of all human endeavour. Or it's more like your mother, daily, routinely, sweeping away the clutter, let's call it debris, we earnestly deposit every waking and sleeping second of our lives. Flesh flakes and dust demons, scaly detritus. Such as that. It accumulates even in a vacuum. It's a big headache for your astronauts."

"I have no astronauts," Karl said, at the same time reminding himself he was still asleep.

"Your mother sang as she swept, her way of bestowing joy onto the grim spectacle, and often, let's say, transgendering—if you'll forgive the word—our affairs into a recognizable paradise. Given your plateau achieved as a noted historian, I expect you recall the melody and lyrics of every song. *Little Girl Blue*, what a spectacularly emotional song! Joe Johnson. Janis Joplin, Chet Baker, she could do them all. And clean that shack! My God! This was before your time but I laboured relentlessly, through forlorn years, building that shack."

Shack?

"A log cabin shack. Yours was a small side room containing an oaken barrel utilized as a bathtub. That barrel had running water hot in winter, cold in summer. We all bathed together, H2O being precious."

Karl was alarmed; his eyes, previously locked tight, now snapped open. "I don't remember any of that. Why are you here?"

"Here? The eternal question, Where is here? Those chubbies who so fascinate you are on to something with that future business. Never mind that Faulkner verity, the past isn't, etc. Why? How would I know? Some rank bastard scattered my ashes throughout the realm. Ashes, I ask you! Can that possibly make any sense? No? Well, the alternatives are gruesome, in any event. I'm going now. Lots of depots to hit and never enough time."

Karl felt he wasn't replete. "Lost my pep," dribbled from his lips in a deliberate mumble. "Talking to yourself does not always signify a fraught psyche," he heard someone say. A lone pyjama-clad body passing along the darkened hall.

Something was missing in his perception of a sustainable reality. His response in earlier times, fame a wearisome shadow, was to find himself by losing himself in ancient *mores*. In "ethica," ethology," "the Mores." In folklore, to put it another way. Dear old Prof. Winter, his Yale mentor, had properly warned that 'if one is liable to be shocked by *any* folkways, he ought not to study folkways at all.' The professor would likely shrug at the current folkways: a gun for every citizen, the war on women, mass annihilation, mass hysteria, celebrity worship, rising waters, becrazed evangelicals, a liberal conscience assailed—the mores as avaricious vultures ever circling. In Deep-in-the-Heart-Of this week they executed by lethal injection this year's one thousandth person. An elite legislative posse was studying why so few were women and children.

"Homer was blind, Beethoven deaf, Maupassant syphilitic, Monet a shrieker. Jesus a wilderness freak!" This the ramrod obese one shouted at Karl. "Virginia Poe, like Lady Gaga, is my ideal. What do you make of them apples, Dr. dipshit hotshot historian?" She was conveying a crippled arm, it perhaps an injury intentionally delivered by experts.

"I slipped on a Slurpee, you poop," she said. "Say! My daddy, a waste management aficionado, claims that women err is believing men prefer the big-titty girl. I mean real bazookas. He says most men want the plum size. The Tea Cup Nellie, he calls them. How's a girl to know? What's the historical view? Mores, that's of Latin derivation. I've checked you out, Dr. Pulitzer-nominated Shit. Is there a willie relationship in this titty crap?"

"What is your real name?" Karl asked.

She paled. She looked truly horrified. "Ja-nine el Diablo," she finally said. "I'll truly fix your engine if you ever get personal with me again. Poof. You're a poof. Dollars to cupcakes, your big bazooka gal Lasalle behoved the identical."

"You talk funny," Karl dared saying.

"It's blimp talk," she said, taking a swing at him with the good arm. "I'm scooting. Deep-dish Decadent Chocolate Pie awaits."

Did those obese cherubs sleep nastily as he did?

Much later in the week Karl was summoned to the public phone. He heard his daughter's voice arche a jubilant hello. "I am in detox," Zulu said. "I have been here all week. You will not believe how depraved we all are. Voices in the head, body lice, bedbugs, bloody lips, mangled ears and noses, that kind of thing. An aged creature drugged to the gills told me today Mathew, Mark, Luke, and John were like failed characters in a Pinter play. If only they did not talk so Much. That is interesting, do you not think? She might more astutely have conjectured Joyce or Beckett as biblical scribes, in my view. Well, they were, some of us might aver. The shrinking bee population is her other obsession. She is forever shrieking, *'Then where will we get our honey?'* I am afflicted by a poisonous radiance but perceived in her light I am a blinding sunbeam. Daddy? Are you there? I fell off the trolley. I made a big, big splash, falling. I was truly horrendous. Like someone sleeping in her own puddle. I cruised through or gave away all my money, then came within an inch of selling myself. So now I am doing penance. I am once again undergoing the renewing process. I soon hope to achieve the vegetative state. In the meanwhile I am a little white mouse in a cage awaiting the developments accorded little white mice of addictive personality. I am dressed today in the little white playsuit addicted little white mice frequently prefer. 'What a darling playsuit!' people may say. 'But where is your sandbox, where is your little blue scoop and nice blue pail?' If we are polite and submissive, if we are good and earn the privilege we are allowed one cigarette twice a week in what is called the Bessie Courtyard. I remember Dr. Bessie and his Bessie wife sometimes came to dinner when we lived on Wilberforce Street and you were Chair. Dr. Bessie might very well be delighted to learn your daughter is fascinatingly encamped in the citadel bearing his name. He was always a gentle, generous soul, is that not so? He liked clipping my chin. I once heard his Bessie wife whispering to a seatmate, 'What awful dresses! Some nice woman should take these dreary girls in hand.' Oh, rot, Daddy! Are you there? Three faux-gold benches depicting charging lions uplift the Bessie Courtyard, each saying in faded script Dr Pepper 10, 2, and 4. Would not we all die? When I get my release I fully intend to sneak into your environs that unerring cognac you crave. I guarantee you an unblemished seal. Your Zulu is desperate for a bath, a manicure and pedicure and a hair stylist who demonically practices her trade. They are clairvoyant, those stylists, they see through to heaven, like those village smithies you liked dotting your literary landscape. 'Blond streaks to lighten your face, give credence to those sexy hips!' they like to say. You cannot possibly know what such coddling means to a daughter low in spirit as a freight car derailed. Not now, I mean, now I'm high and dry, sailing over the treetops of a roofless world. Do you remember the Man in my Life? The Nowhere Man? Ask him where he has been and he says Nowhere. It must be a wonderful place, that Nowhere. All my beaus went there. By the way, why I am calling, how is that amnesia of yours coming along? Is it in overdrive? Is it a four-gear or five-gear model, pedal to the floor? Will you buy me a new automobile if I remain good? My vintage Desoto died of a heart attack. Spots on the lungs, cardiovascular disassociation, hardened arteries, malady of that ilk. That Desoto you gave me on my sixteenth was older than the twelfth-century pope, whosit, you wrote your first book about. Celestine V, that is the name. The hermit pope who perished from a nail driven through his head. Am I refreshing your brain? Did the nail arrive while old Celestine was alive or was it implanted during one of his endless reburials? Such was your quandary. I recall my excitement upon discovering a full signature of pages where you assumed the point of view of the nail. Gertrude Stein could not have done better. Those silver coffins stolen over and over, then his remains usurped in the bargain. I memorized that book, you will recall, reciting it to pianola accompaniment and the clink of after-dinner drinks. I believe you were hospitalized when not long ago Celestine's remains were discovered beneath Abruzzo earthquake rubble. The nail still intact. Oh, Lord, those popes! I wonder if you recall the lovely poem you wrote for me when I was six, about a tribe in Paraguay, the Kadiveo and their cousins the Guykurus, whose women spent nearly their entire fertile lives on horseback so as to hinder the conception of children. It does not work, you told me; the riding, not the poem. Gee, I loved to the moon that poem. An AB AB rhyme scheme, fluid in the middle. Free verse, that captive bird released, orphaned to the wild, you explained. But Daddy? Are you there? Are you hanging in? The sanguine why behind this call has pertinence to that woman you call Ishmael—Lasalle, I mean. Is—*forgive me!*—is she my true mother? Is she? Would she have loved me?"

Often now when Karl reflected on this troubled daughter, one of three uncanny spirits haunting the universe, he visualized a solitary carrier pigeon, intent and disciplined, feathers tattered, combatting high peaks and baffling winds, thinking, in concert with every flash of star, "Ah, the mystery."

All three were tightly packed as mangos, and twice as slippery.

Long, long ago, when this trinity still were children and it was this one's birthday, they had sat down to a candlelit dinner in a sunken garden somewhere in the south of France. At their insistence, sardines in olive oil, saltines. and canned pork and beans the sole fare. *Gifts for you, my lovely girls!* Each still wore, on thin silver chains, the tiny pendants around their necks. A fifth party had been present, surely. Lasalle?

"I look forward greedily to the simple life," said the birthday girl, "though I waft a fragrant perfume."

The sun waned. Throughout the day it waned and waned. It knew not what else to do. Karl thought of it as a yearning sun, wanting to go where suns never had ventured before. It wanted to bed the moon but the moon only turned the cold shoulder. Karl's eyelids became sticky, looking at that amazing sun. He requested permission to limp down to that establishment where one could secure alcoholic nourishment. In rather strident terms the request was denied. That privilege requires five stars, he was told. You have barely scratched the board.

The board, in any case, was constantly being defaced. It was a sphinx of obscenity defining a mores peculiar to the time and place.

Karl spent many hours observing the vista-deprived window. Each day something new was to be seen sliding down the glass— grapefruit remains, oatmeal, yogurt. Animal entrails. Someone had attempted painting on the window a green treescape in which sat a dwarfed cabin, smoke billowing from the chimney, but the glass rejected this initiative. An edict was circulated, giving rise to heart-rending depression among staff and patient alike: the obese girls had been separated, shipped off to undisclosed wings.

Hunger strikes were predicted. Waterboarding threatened.

Scottish Annie
Alice Petersen

On Saturdays at five Archie McLean visits the retirement home to take requests at the piano. Each week the seniors try to trip him. "Robins and Roses," they'll say, naming some old tune that they used to dance to on the wind-up. But they can't catch Archie out. Archie knows them all and he sings in that old fashioned radio way, leaning back on the piano stool, nodding to the ladies. Then at the end he opens the piano lid right up and plays an extra fast bumblebee song. I'm usually out in the garden when Archie gets back after the tea and scones, and then he leans over the hedge to tell me about it.

"Well Ruby," says Archie, "I think we wowed them today." It always makes me laugh. You would think he was a whole orchestra the way he talks. Archie is a nice young man. Genteel, my mother would have said. We play scrabble on Wednesday nights. He's been my neighbour for nearly fifteen years now. Back in March he celebrated his fiftieth birthday, and I made an eggless chocolate cake, because Archie doesn't believe in exploiting the hens. He served me a slice and said so when's your birthday, Ruby? I said get away with you, a lady doesn't admit to her age until she's in for a telegram from the Queen. All I'm saying is I'm not old enough to be your mother. Have some more cake.

Last week, when he had finished toting up the score for the word *umbilical*, Archie told me that he has to move, because his landlord wants to sell the house. I was very sorry to hear that. Archie has been a great friend to me.

After mother died, three years ago next February, Archie got me started volunteering at the retirement home as well. He said it was better than hiding in the potting shed. At the time I said that I wasn't hiding and that I'd think about it. Now I take the seniors out on wee trips in the car. Archie is the piano man and I am the driving juke box. They tell me where they want to go, and I take them, within four hours and within reason. Often they like to go back to where they were born, or where they've had picnics in the past. One afternoon I drove 90-year-old Willy Callaghan to Oamaru. We idled outside a renovated villa on Vine Street while Mr. Callaghan wept for the loss of the corrugated iron sheets on the roof and the front room where he had been born. I said that a nice conservatory full of tomatoes was nothing to cry about. Still, I let him have a good old weep, and then we went for an ice cream and came home. It takes me a year to get through all of the seniors, so some of the older ones don't come more than once.

When I arrived up at the home last week, Mrs. Webster was waiting for me in the foyer, all wrapped up warm for her outing. She always wears mohair cardies that her niece from up Ranfurly way knits for her. The light catches in the hairs.

"You're glowing, Mrs. Webster," I said, and she was pleased. Mohair keeps your chest warm, but it's not cheap, and it gets stringy. Better to mix it with a bit of wool. "Anyway," I said, "where are we off to today?" Mrs. Webster wanted to go to the nursery at Blueskin Bay, to buy a miniature rose for her bedroom. She had a coupon from the paper. They do love coupons. So off we went, out through Pine Hill and over the motorway to the nursery. She got a wee apricot rose to match her curtains. I almost got one too, but then I thought it was silly to get over excited about plants that don't survive the winter.

Mrs. Webster was sitting in the car looking at the little rose bush on her lap. Then she looked at me quite shyly.

"Do you think we could take the road along the coast, through Seacliff?" she asked.

"Of course we can, Mrs. Webster," I said. "My wish is your command." So away we went, winding along above the sea past the rabbit holes in the yellow clay banks and the twisted macrocarpa trees along the fence lines.

"Seacliff always makes me sad," I said, just to make conversation. It's the kind of thing that people say when they drive

165

through Seacliff. The paddocks there fall so steeply toward the sea that it's hard to tell how a sheep might hold on in the wind, let alone a farmer on a bike. And you think you might hear some ghost from the asylum wailing away in the breeze. It was a grand old place, the asylum at Seacliff, majestic and crenellated. They had proper lunatics in those days.

"Just here, Ruby dear, drive me up here," said Mrs. Webster, "up toward the asylum, to those trees at the top of the road." We stopped by a gate where there was nothing to see, just an old car with no head lights, buried in the bushes, and pile of bricks to show where a house once stood.

"I was born here," said Mrs. Webster. "The back door faced the asylum, and the verandah ran all around the house. And up the hill under the eucalyptus trees there were passion fruit vines with purple flowers, all fringed with blue. Every year Mum would take us up to look at the flowers, and she would say, 'See kids, even in Seacliff.' And we would say, 'even in Seacliff what, Mum?' And she always replied, 'even in Seacliff we can be on a tropical island.' She had a lovely laugh, our Mum."

"Shall we walk up and have a look Mrs. Webster?" I said. "Would you like that?" I helped her out of the car and into her coat, found her stick, took her arm. The wind was fierce. Together we took granny steps up the paddock toward the gum trees at the top.

"My mother was known as Scottish Annie," said Mrs. Webster. "She had that kind of bone china skin that reddens in the southerly wind. She used to stand on the porch shading her eyes with her hand, looking out at the sea, while she sent my sister Milly to get the washing in, 'quicksticks, before the rain comes.' It was a deal of work to keep the five of us washed and mended I can tell you. She did the washing on a Saturday, which was considered quite unusual, but that way the boys could help. Johnnie stirred the copper with a big stick. Our Mum didn't do things quite like other people."

Mrs. Webster was looking way out across the ocean. I could tell that she had a story to tell so I let her run. So many of the older ones only have fragments left, but that afternoon Mrs. Webster could still put her hand on the whole thing.

"Our Dad was killed by a coal dray coming down Stafford Street," said Mrs Webster. "Dad rolled right out of the pub and into the road and then the dray came clattering down the hill, and that was that. You might think that the coal merchant would have had the decency to send a load out to the widow, but he didn't.

Mum let out the paddocks to Mr. Currie to run his cows on. The cows used to come up and look at us through the window. Then our Mum got a job serving hot dinner up at the asylum, but that still wasn't enough, so we got a lodger. His name was Mr. Reginald Hooper. Mr. Hooper was a clean-cut medical resident, neat as a pin, with round spectacles that he polished with a handkerchief that came out of his pocket, and such nice clean nails. He must have wondered what had happened to him, coming into our house with five kids roaring about. But he never said anything and he was as polite as you please, and out of the house early and not back until tea time. We had our tea first, and then Mum would give the lodger his stew and tell us to go away and let the man have his dinner in peace, because he worked in the madhouse all day and he didn't have to live in one too. We called him Mr. Hooper, but Johnnie sometimes called him Dr. Whooping Cough. We thought that was terribly funny.

Mr. Hooper did his best to be handy about the house, even though Mum would never have asked him to lift a finger. A couple of the big eucalyptus trees up the back had been cut down and when Mr. Hooper came home in the evening he would chop his heart out with his sleeves rolled up and his dark hair flopping about. The first wood pile he made came down in the night. How we laughed. Mr. Hooper bit his lip and went out in the dark to stack it again. He liked to bring a load in and put it by the stove ready to use, and our Mum didn't have the heart to tell him that it would take six months to get the wood half dry enough for burning.

Mr. Hooper was nice to us kids too, and he didn't have to be. He brought in gum nuts and put them in a box for the baby to shake. And once, when he saw us watching him put his boots on, he turned his sock into a snake that spoke in a funny voice, and another time he did a shadow show on the wall with his hands—you know, the dove, the old woman, the Turk—all those shapes he could do.

After dinner Mr. Hooper studied his medical books at the kitchen table. Our Mum sat in the cane chair with the sock basket on her knees, darning and watching him work. She made him a pot of tea, but she wouldn't take a cup herself. She was so proud to have Dr. Whooping Cough and his white coat staying at our house. She put him to sleep in the parlour! How people talked. It was cold in the front parlour. That's why Mr. Hooper studied his books in the kitchen.

The four older kids, Frankie, Millie, Johnnie, and Meggie, went to school, but at the beginning the baby went down the road to Mrs. Wren's. Then Mrs. Wren's back got bad and baby couldn't go there any more. So in the mornings our Mum would put the baby in the pen containing the vegetable garden, plump down on its bottom among the cabbages. Every so often she would nip outside to shake out a rag and sing out tralaloo, just to check that the baby was alright. She must have been shaking out the rags every two minutes.

One morning while the older kids were at school and the baby was in the pen in the back yard, the kitchen chimney caught fire. All that resin from the green wood had built up in the dog leg of the flue. Well that's what Mr. Currie said later. He had warned our Mum, but the flue caught fire. It smouldered for a long time and then it got roaring hot. Our Mum had left her apron hung over the fire guard in the kitchen and the gum nuts in the pockets cracked open in the heat.

Mr. Currie was on his way up the hill to look at Dolores who had hoof rot. He smelt the smoke and ran to the house. And I saw the fire too, because I was that baby, you know. It's one of my earliest memories, poking a stick at a piece of wood where the paint has swelled up into lovely soft bubbles. Mr. Currie ran into the burning house and he found our Mum and the lodger passed out on the bed. Entwined they were. At noon. And her not even wearing a wrapper. Mr. Currie had to get it off the hook on the back of the door. First he brought our Mum out, and then Mr. Currie, such a brave man, went back in for Mr. Hooper. After that there was nothing that could be done to save the house. Dry as tinder it was under the rafters. You must have been able to see the flames far out at sea.

Mr. Currie laid Mum and Mr. Hooper side by side on the cold grass and covered them with a blanket. And the hill beside the house there is so steep that the bodies were almost standing up. Carbon monoxide had come creeping up on them. Well. They came round eventually. No harm done, and everyone said that it was a miracle. Even Mr. Currie said that, because if they had both died, who would have looked after all those kids?

Well, Mr. Hooper did the decent thing, and he married our Mum, took her on with the five kids and even had another one. That's my younger brother Neil. He's up in the Ross Home now. And Mr. Hooper's parents, they also did the decent thing and they disowned him. And you can be sure that no-one at Seacliff was going to let Scottish Annie have her cake and eat it too, dandling her young man in the bedroom while the house burned down and the baby sat in the back yard with The Lord Knows What in its mouth. So our Mum sold the paddocks and we all moved to Caversham, to a wee house in the shade of the hill. Mr. Hooper got work filling orders in a chemist's shop. But he would not let our Mum go to work, no he would not. She was his queen. Queen of the washboard, more like, but in those days, men were proud and they didn't want their women to work.

For a long time we had nothing at all, except swedes, boiled and mashed and roasted. But my step father was a good man. I never saw his belt buckle coming my way and that's a lot more than the older ones could say for our Dad. Mr. Hooper was the only Dad I ever knew. So it's not just sorrow that comes out of Seacliff. It was good for us kids, at any rate until the war came. But that wasn't just us. That was everybody."

By the time she finished talking, Mrs. Webster and I were back in the car, fussing with the seatbelts, trying to get our hands warm. Heading back into town I wanted to say to her, but you were the baby—if you can't remember the bodies laid out on the grass and the passion fruit flower sitting in a cup of water on the kitchen table, then how do you know that it happened that way? But the story is true. Mrs. Webster knows it by heart. You can tell. And I could not bother her with questions, because she had fallen asleep. That's how it is so often with these trips in the car. Clear as a bell, like a song in all its verses, and then their eye lids come down and the story is finished.

I don't mind letting on that I envied Mrs. Webster her story. I would have liked a large family and a life rounded out with pots of tea, biscuits and chat at the kitchen table. But Mother always said that I could not expect much with my blunt features and heavy bones. Not that any of it matters now, at my age, no matter what the magazines say.

Still, I have a good mind to ask Archie if he would like to take the granny flat at the bottom of the garden. It has a brand new refrigerator that never saw more than a bottle of milk because Mother took all her meals with me. I rather fancy the sound of the piano coming up from behind the buddleia. He could have the folding card table and Mother's extra chairs. We could make tea and play scrabble on Wednesday nights. He could be a proper lodger.

Oh I know you're thinking that I'm after Archie, but you'd be wrong, for Archie McLean is not the marrying kind. No, it's just that after I've passed on, I'd rather like it if one person, and maybe it might be Archie, would stop the car outside my bungalow, smile at the upturned faces of the marigolds, and say, yes, happy times we had there, happy times.

MARK ANTHONY JARMAN has published five collections of stories, *Dancing Nightly in the Tavern, New Orleans Is Sinking, 19 Knives, My White Planet* and *Knife Party at the Hotel Europa*, a collection of poetry, *Killing the Swan*, a novel, *Salvage King Ya!* and a travel book, *Ireland's Eye*. He is the fiction editor of *The Fiddlehead* and teaches at UNB.

KERRY-LEE POWELL has lived in Antigua, Australia and the UK. Her work has won numerous awards, including *The Boston Review* fiction contest, *The Malahat Review* Far Horizons award, and the Alfred G. Bailey manuscript prize. Her first book of poetry, *Inheritance*, was published in 2014.

REBECCA ROSENBLUM has published two collections of short stories, *Once* and *The Big Dream*, and a chapbook, *Road Trips*. A novel, *So Much Love,* is forthcoming. She lives, works and writes in Toronto with her husband, the author Mark Sampson.

ADRIAN MICHAEL KELLY is the author of a novel, *Down Sterling Road*, and a forthcoming collection of short fiction, *The Ambassador of What*. His stories have appeared in *Best Canadian Stories* and *The Journey Prize Stories*, as well as in *TNQ, Prairie Fire* and other periodicals. He currently lives in Genoa.

KATHY PAGE has published seven novels and two collections of stories, and has been a runner-up for the Governor General's Award, the Giller Prize, the Ethel Wilson Prize and the Orange Prize. Born in England, she moved to Salt Spring Island in 2001. A third story collection, *The Two of Us*, will appear in 2016.

CYNTHIA FLOOD is the author of a novel, *Making a Stone of the Heart*, and four books of short fiction, the most recent of which is *Red Girl Rat Boy*, a runner-up for the Ethel Wilson Fiction Prize and the Frank O'Connor Award. Her stories have previously won both a National Magazine Award and the Journey Prize. She lives in Vancouver.

LAUREN CARTER is the author of *Swarm*, named by the CBC as one of the Top 40 novels that could change Canada, and *Lichen Bright*, a collection of poetry. She currently lives in The Pas, Manitoba, where she writes a popular weekly blog on life and writing at www.laurencarter.ca.

MEGAN FINDLAY has published stories in *The New Quarterly*, *Canadian Notes & Queries*, *The Feathertale Review* and *Encore*. She has been shortlisted for the CBC Literary Award and in 2015 was a finalist for the National Magazine Awards. She lives in Ottawa.

KEVIN HARDCASTLE has appeared in *The Malahat Review*, *PRISM international*, *The New Quarterly* and *Event*, and his work has been selected twice for *The Journey Prize Stories*. A story collection, *Debris*, will be published in 2015. He grew up in Simcoe County but now lives in Toronto.

LEON ROOKE will publish his seventeenth story collection in 2016. His first novel, *Fat Woman*, appeared in 1980, and was shortlisted for the Governor General's Award. Many others have followed, most recently *The Beautiful Wife*. He has also published poetry and stage plays, and his paintings are widely held. He lives in Toronto.

ALICE PETERSEN grew up in New Zealand. Her stories have been shortlisted for the Journey Prize, the Writers' Union of Canada Competition and the CBC Literary Award. Her first collection, *All the Voices Cry*, won the QWF first book award. A second collection, *Worldly Goods*, will appear in 2016.

JOHN METCALF is one of Canada's best-known editors. He was born in England in 1938, emigrated to Montreal in 1962 and currently lives in Ottawa with his wife Myrna. In 2004 he was made a member of the Order of Canada. His most recent books are *Shut Up He Explained*, a memoir, and *Standing Stones*, a collection of selected stories.